The Stepsisters

#7 Reckless Sister

Tina Oaks

SCHOLASTIC INC.
New York Toronto London Auckland Sydney

ISBN 0-590-41872-6

12 11 10 9 8 7 6 5 4 3 2 1 8 9/8 0 1 2 3/9

Printed in the U.S.A. 01

First Scholastic printing, August 1988

Reckless Sister

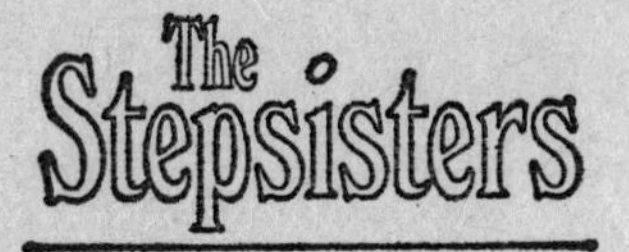

The War Between the Sisters
The Sister Trap
Bad Sisters
Sisters in Charge
That Cheating Sister
Guilty Sister
Reckless Sister

CHAPTER 1

Paige Whitman hurried around the room she shared with her stepsister, Katie Summer Guthrie, hunting for earrings, shoes, and panty hose. She muttered to herself as she propelled her tall, slim body from one cramped, cluttered corner to another. Long, dark hair swung beside her narrow face as she moved.

"If you'd put things where they belong when you finish with them," Katie pointed out, "you wouldn't go through this frantic ritual every time you go out." She shook her blonde head disapprovingly, and added in a murmur, "And our room wouldn't look like C.I.A. agents had been in here searching for hidden microphones."

She was lying on her own bed, comfortable in a pink sweat suit, munching on an apple. "I don't know what you and Mom see in these concerts, anyway. Sitting through two hours of classical music sounds like Chinese water torture to me." Her lovely face contorted in a grimace of distaste.

Paige located the missing earrings. They were hiding in a crumpled tissue on her half of the dresser's surface. She called their room the House of Dr. Jekyll and Ms. Hyde because Katie's half was immaculate while her own was anything but. Fastening the earrings, she said in a superior tone of voice, "I've always felt sorry for people who don't understand or appreciate the finer things in life."

Katie looked amused. "Such as?"

"Such as classical music. That stuff you listen to will make you deaf as a post before you reach the age of thirty, a mere fifteen years from now."

Katie laughed. "You sound exactly like Mom! And you listen to 'that stuff,' too, and you know it." She didn't feel like saying so, but Paige looked really great in a full-length black velvet skirt and a deep cherry red long-sleeved top with a scoop neckline. She seldom dressed up, but when she did, Katie decided, she looked stunning. Especially when she arranged her hair in a twist at the back of her neck, as she was doing now, brushing it straight back from her face and long, graceful neck.

"Well, your mother happens to be right," Paige said, bending from the waist to brush every last strand of hair up and back. "Maybe you should listen to her. And I do *not* listen to that stuff!"

Katie hated it when Paige united herself with Virginia Mae, like they were partners or something. It was bad enough that Paige was older, by one year, than she was. And it was bad enough that she, who had been raised to believe that "everything has a proper place" was now sharing a room with a compulsive pack-rat. But the worst, the absolute *worst*, was the fact that her stepsister and her mother got along so well. They shared a love of music (which included a mutual talent at the piano) and they both loved to write. Virginia Mae Guthrie Whitman, mother to Tucker, Katie Summer, and Mary Emily Guthrie, stepmother to Paige and Megan Whitman, had been a respected journalist in Atlanta, Georgia, before her marriage to Philadelphia attorney William Whitman, and Paige now worked on the school newspaper. Those were bonds Katie felt she couldn't compete with, and Paige's smug attitude about her relationship with Virginia Mae just made it worse.

"Anyway," Paige said, putting the finishing touches on her hair, "it's not the concert I'm excited about as much as the party afterwards. Oh, the concert will be great. They're doing two of my favorite pieces. But this party isn't a high-school event, with everyone spilling soda all over the place and telling stupid jokes."

Katie raised her eyebrows.

"This," Paige continued, slipping her feet into black leather flats, "is a *grown-up* party, for charity. They're going to serve champagne." She turned to face Katie Summer, her dark eyes shining, her cheeks bright with excitement. "And Mom said I could have some."

Katie still hadn't become accustomed to the sound of the word "Mom" on Paige's lips when she was referring to Virginia Mae. And she still wanted to say, "She's not your mother, she's mine." She suspected that Paige felt exactly the same way when Katie called Paige's father, "Dad."

Envy washed over her as she watched Paige apply a touch of blusher to high cheekbones. The party *did* sound like fun. And she *had* been invited and could have gone. She had chosen to pass on the occasion, knowing the concert would bore her. Paige never came to any of her swim meets, for the very same reason. "Swimming in competition just looks so . . . damp!" she had said once.

"You look really nice," Katie said sincerely.

Never one to respond well to a compliment, Paige flushed. "Oh. Well, I probably should have curled my hair but it wouldn't stay curled, so what's the point?" But she did turn back toward the closet door mirror for one last look.

Katie admired the graceful way Paige moved. It would be difficult, if not impossible, for anyone who didn't know to guess that Paige had only recently recovered from a serious car accident that had nearly taken her life and had done major damage to her right leg. Surgery, time in traction, and physical therapy had followed, leaving the entire family drained and exhausted. Katie, who had been driving the car but was totally blameless, had worked her way through the inescapable guilt with difficulty. And now, watching Paige move about the room almost effortlessly, with the tiniest hint of a limp, she said a quiet prayer of thanks that this terrible episode in their lives was behind them.

"Maybe I'll meet someone scrumptious tonight," Paige said, throwing a black velvet blazer over her shoulders.

Katie frowned. "You already *have* someone scrumptious. I think Ben is really neat."

She was referring to Ben Collins, the tall, thin, bespectacled co-editor of the school newspaper. He was a serious student, whom Katie found to be kind and understanding. And she knew that, although Ben himself might have trouble saying so, he genuinely cared about Paige.

"Oh, sure, Ben's great! But we're not engaged or anything, Katie. Ben doesn't own me. And if I look as nice as you say I do," she said, grinning, "who knows what might happen?"

"You *do* look nice," Katie said generously. "You really do."

Satisfied with that, Paige picked up a small black clutch purse from her bed and left the room.

Katie rolled over on her back and lay staring up at the ceiling. How blissfully quiet the room seemed with Paige absent! Paige's messy clutter remained, but Katie could close her eyes to that and enjoy the peace. She missed having her own room. It was different for Mary Emily, her ten-year-old sister, who seemed tickled pink to have a brand-new sister her own age in Megan. They had had no problems at all in sharing a room. Maybe, Katie reflected soberly, maybe it was just very different when you were only ten. She had, once upon a time, looked forward to having a new sister, too. That seemed ages ago now, though it it was only months. Her excitement and optimism at the prospect of having a whole new family had quickly been shot down by the arrival in Atlanta of a stiff-necked, prickly Paige. She wouldn't even meet me halfway, Katie thought. She'd already made up her mind that we southern girls are useless, dim-witted, hopeless flirts. Katie giggled softly. I *am* a flirt, and that's the truth. But so are most of the girls at school and they're *not* southern. Anyway, Paige is wrong about the other things. I'm *not* useless, and I'm as bright as she is, when I work at it.

The front door slammed. She thought about running to the window to watch her parents and Paige leave, and then realized it was too dark to see anything outside. Her mother, whom she had passed in the hallway earlier, had looked lovely in a long peach gown with lace trim. Her stepfather, resplendent in a tuxedo, tall and broad-shouldered, slightly graying at the temples, made the perfect escort for Virginia Mae. How lucky for her mother, alone for such a long time after Katie's father left, to find a warm, loving husband like Bill Whitman.

But whenever Katie mentioned, in Paige's presence, how romantic it all was, all she got in return was a cynical half-smile and a muttered comment that sounded suspiciously like, "hopelessly dippy girl!"

The knock on her bedroom door belonged unmistakably to her seventeen-year-old brother,

Tuck. He always knocked in a commanding way, as if he couldn't conceive of anyone denying him entry. When she called, "Come in!" he opened the door and stuck his curly head into the room. He had delicate features like his mother, but a strong jaw that told of his stubborn tenacity. And he had a wonderful, crooked grin, although Katie noticed more and more often that he grinned less and less.

"Another long-hair music night for the folks, hmm?" he commented. "You got any plans?"

She hoped *he* did. Tuck's adjustment from south to north had been more difficult than his sisters'. A polite, dignified "southern gentleman" like Tuck didn't fit in all that easily at raucous, free-wheeling Harrison High. If he wasn't being teased about his easy drawl, he was being faulted for the fine manners his mother had instilled in him. Katie knew it was hard for him, not being one of the guys as he had been in Atlanta, but at least he was still trying. And he seemed to be making some progress with the girl of his choice, the beautiful, popular Jennifer Bailey. Although Ms. Bailey seemed to have a problem unlatching herself from Harrison High's star quarterback, the thick-skulled Ed Thomas, she *was* also being seen with Tucker Guthrie. Katie couldn't help wondering about Jennifer's taste in men. It seemed to her that if a light bulb went on over Ed Thomas's head every time he spoke, it would surely only be a ten-watt bulb. Maybe Jennifer was just finding old habits hard to break.

She shrugged. "Maybe Jake will drop by later. You going out?"

He grinned. It was such a nice grin. But then, Katie told herself, Tucker Guthrie was a nice guy. She wished he were happier with this new life of theirs. "Meeting Jennifer after the game. How come you didn't go? You and your pals usually drag the old school spirit over to the stadium."

"Sara's visiting her grandparents this weekend, Lisa's got a cold, and Diane's got a date. I thought you were going, though."

He made a face of distaste. "Not me. Football's not my game, you know that. All those Hulks knocking each other silly over a lump of pigskin just makes me want to laugh."

She knew what he really meant. He couldn't stand the fuss made over Ed Thomas, who was a superior athlete. Katie decided he couldn't possibly be as stupid as she thought he was, or he wouldn't succeed as quarterback. That took brains. Maybe he wasn't stupid. Maybe a more accurate description would be . . . crass . . . vulgar.

She nodded. "Right. Well, have fun. I'm just going to lie here like a slug and wait for the doorbell to ring." With a grin, she added, "Kindly notice I am now the only occupant of this room. Isn't that great? Peace . . . it's wonderful!"

Tuck made no comment. She knew how much he hated the bickering that went on between her and Paige. Their relationship wasn't at all what he'd expected it to be. She also knew he blamed the two of them for creating so much tension in the yellow Victorian house high on a hill. She shouldn't have expressed her delight at being alone.

"Paige sure looked great tonight, didn't she?" he asked.

Good old Tuck! He never gave up. He wanted so much for them to be one big, happy Beaver Cleaver family. Did he really think prodding her into complimenting Paige would solve all their problems? And did he really think she was so petty that she wouldn't have complimented Paige on her own, without being prodded?

"Yes, she did," Katie answered. "I told her so, twice," a hint of defiance in her voice.

Tuck couldn't hide the look of surprise on his face. "Oh. Great. Well, look, I'll see you later. I hope Jake doesn't disappoint you."

Katie was fairly sure he wouldn't. She waved to Tuck as he closed the door. Then again, she told herself, you just never know with Jake. Periodically bothered by the fact that he was eighteen and she was only fifteen ("and a half," she reminded him often), he would sometimes, without warning, back away from their relationship. Still, one of the gratifying things about this move north was that Jake had come with the house, so to speak. Taking a year off between high school and college, with an eye toward law school, Jake served as handyman/yard man to the Whitmans. Tall and solid, with a strong, rugged face, and a thick shock of dark hair, Jake had been drawn to Katie from the minute he'd seen her . . . and she had felt the same way.

How could she have known that she wasn't the only member of the household who was attracted to Jake? Still, being perfectly honest meant admitting that even if she *had* known her stepsister dreamed of Jake Carson at night, even if she *had* known that beginning a relationship with him would mean sabotaging the one she was beginning with Paige, she would still have introduced herself to Jake on that first day. Anything else was unthinkable.

But Paige had never forgiven her. Katie had thought that dating Ben would take Paige's mind off Jake, but there were times when she wasn't at all sure how Paige really felt about Ben. Like tonight, when Paige had made that remark about meeting someone "scrumptious" at the party after the concert. That didn't sound like something someone in love would say.

Katie got up to comb her hair and go downstairs. The housekeeper, Miss Aggie, had gone home for the day, and Mary Emily and Megan were playing in their room. That left no one downstairs to answer the doorbell and Katie wasn't taking any chances on Jake thinking no one was home and leaving. Hurrying down the stairs, she found herself hoping that her parents were having a good time. And, wanting to be fair, that Paige was, too.

Paige was having a good time. She had discovered, among the members of the Symphony orchestra, a face she'd never seen before. She wasn't sure if she had noticed him because he was new to the group, or because he was so attractive, with high cheekbones and dark hair, a few strands falling across his forehead as he pulled the bow across his cello. He was lost in the music, an intense expression on his face, his full mouth set in concentration.

She had no idea who he was. But whoever he was, if he showed up at the party she was going to meet him. Whatever that took, she would do it. Because she wasn't going home tonight without finding out more about the young man who lost himself in music, the same way she did.

CHAPTER 2

A group of tuxedoed musicians arrived at the party five minutes after Paige and her parents got there. The cellist, laughing, was in the center of the group. Paige, standing in the ballroom of the hotel, leaning against a long table covered in expensive linen and bearing a huge crystal punch bowl and trays and platters of food, felt her knees grow weak. What a wonderful laugh this cellist had!

If Paige had had any idea how lovely she looked, standing alone under the glow of a brilliantly-lit crystal chandelier, she wouldn't have lost her breath in shock when he looked in her direction, stopped in his tracks and, smiling, advanced directly toward her. Even then, she told herself he was probably very thirsty after hours of sitting under the hot lights on the stage, and that delighted expression on his face came from the prospect of helping himself at the punch bowl.

But it wasn't the punch bowl he was addressing as he thrust out a hand and said, "Hello, there! Philip Taylor Grant, at your service. And who might you be?"

Paige realized with horror that she had lost her ability to speak. And that it didn't matter, because even if she had been able to speak, she had also forgotten her name.

"Something wrong?" he asked, concern in his voice. His eyes were dark, as she had known they would be, and seemed to peer right through her. His hair was longish, curling slightly just above the collar of his tuxedo jacket. She thought that very romantic and appropriate for a musician.

"What?" he asked as she struggled frantically to regain her powers of speech, "you don't like musicians? Is that it?"

"Oh, I *love* musicians," she burst out, and then, mortified, quickly added, "I mean, I love *music*!"

"Well, of course you do, or you wouldn't be here, would you?" He filled a cup with punch and handed it to her. "So you do speak, after all. Good." He took her elbow and gently led her over to a quiet corner embellished with a large ficus tree in a giant brass pot, flanked by three white iron chairs, cushioned in gold velvet. "You and I are going to talk," he said, softly.

She sat down, holding the cup carefully to avoid spilling red liquid on her velvet skirt. She felt . . . not quite there, as if some other girl had taken a seat next to this smiling, handsome young man, and she was just watching from a distance.

"Do you have a name? I'd hate to have to say, Hey, you! It's so rude, don't you think?"

Paige, who had been staring into her cup, looked up, startled. "What? Oh." She sat up straighter, vowing to stop acting like a ninny. Wasn't this exactly what she had hoped for? "Of course I have a name. It's Paige. Paige Whitman. I'm here with my parents." She hadn't meant to say that. Now he'd think she was just a child, unable to venture forth alone after dark. She hastened to add, "They're supporters of the Symphony."

He nodded his approval. A young man approached and moved toward the third chair. Paige's companion cleared his throat deeply and gave the newcomer a fierce frown. The young man took the hint and left.

Pulling his chair closer to hers, the cellist said, "Well, I'm Philip. The Taylor is my mother's maiden name and the Grant is my father's last name."

Paige laughed, noticing with satisfaction that her hand on the punch cup was perfectly steady.

"I'm originally from Ohio. I'm currently guest cellist for your Symphony. I'm an only child; I travel a lot; I like to cook; and I'm twenty-one years old."

Oh-oh. He wasn't about to ask *her* age, was he? He obviously hadn't guessed correctly or he wouldn't be sitting here now, would he?

"Music is my great love," he continued in a light tone of voice, "more important than French fries or football or the global financial situation.

I'm not rich. Musicians seldom are. But I do all right. I don't own a car because I hate driving, but I can afford cab fare and an occasional meal at a restaurant where the chef knows food shouldn't be fried unless absolutely necessary, which is just about never." He fastened his dark eyes on Paige's, and she found herself unable to look away. "And I intend to take you to another charity ball tomorrow night, at a different hotel."

Paige yanked together all the little scattered bits of her composure and was able to say calmly, "Okay."

Delight mixed with the surprise on his handsome face. "You mean it?"

She nodded. "But don't you have a performance?"

He shook his head. "There's a benefit tomorrow afternoon for kids under twelve. I'm playing then. So the regular cellist is doing the honors tomorrow night. You're not otherwise occupied?"

She had a date with Ben. "No, I'm not," she said, telling herself it wasn't really a fib because she had every intention of breaking her date with Ben, which meant that she *wouldn't* be "otherwise occupied." She'd worry about what excuse she was going to give Ben tomorrow.

What might be a lot more complicated was what she was going to tell her parents. Going to a charity ball with them was one thing. Attending the same kind of event with a twenty-one-year-old almost-stranger was another. Virginia Mae would get "that look" on her face, the one Paige still resented, even though she loved her stepmother a lot. But still, she was *not* Paige's real mother. Virginia Mae would strongly disapprove of a person breaking a date at the last minute, and she'd probably have a real fit when she found out Paige was dating someone over eighteen.

But, catching Philip's eyes on her, she decided very quickly that she would think of something. Because she *was* going to that dance with Philip Taylor Grant the following night, no matter what it took.

"Now," he said, settling back in his chair, "tell me about Paige Whitman."

As she struggled frantically to find the correct words to hide the truth without actually lying to him, she found herself wishing Katie Summer could see her now. "You see?" she could hear herself saying proudly, "they don't come much more scrumptious than this!" Wherever Katie was right now, she couldn't possibly be having as interesting an evening as her stepsister.

Katie might have argued that. Jake had indeed shown up, and was at that very moment sitting on the cream-colored sofa in the living room of the Whitman home, with a very contented Katie in his arms. Megan and Mary Emily were watching television in their room, and everyone else was still out for the evening. And Katie Summer was exactly where she wanted to be.

Katie Summer thought of herself as being fairly strong and independent, so she sometimes questioned why, then, leaning on Jake felt so good, so right. The answer was always the same:

Leaning on someone physically, feeling the closeness, was a good thing, while depending on someone else for all the answers, never making up your own mind, was not good. She tried not to do that with Jake. She suspected that he wouldn't let her even if she were silly enough to try letting him run her life. Besides, she'd worked so hard at convincing Jake that she was old enough for him, she had no intention of suddenly turning into a helpless, childish dolt. She would hate that even more than he would.

"Think you'll feel like taking in a movie tomorrow night?" Jake asked, his voice lazy. "Maybe Paige and Ben will decide to tag along."

Remembering Paige's earlier remark about meeting someone new, Katie said she would ask. After all, what were the chances that Paige would meet someone nicer than Ben? Close to zilch, she'd bet.

"You look especially gorgeous tonight, you know that?" Jake said softly. She didn't bat her eyes and blush. She was a flirt, but she seldom played games with Jake. He had no patience for it. Besides, he was too special. She turned toward him and nestled against his chest, murmuring a simple, "Thanks. I'm glad you think so." These were the times she loved most: private, peaceful times with Jake, when family problems, school and swim team hassles all faded away like bad dreams, leaving only the glow of her feelings for him. He hadn't mentioned their age difference in a while, and she sensed that he wasn't going to tonight.

"Want to watch TV?" he asked, his chin in her hair.

"No," she answered honestly. "But we need music. I'll take care of it, okay?"

"Do you have to leave me to take care of it?"

She nodded.

"Then no music," spoken in a firm voice. "You're not moving from here."

Katie laughed softly. "No music? Paige would disapprove. She's at a concert right this very minute."

"Yeah, but we're *not*. And why don't you turn around so I can see those drop-dead blue eyes of yours? I'm tired of talking to the back of your head."

But when she turned around, he didn't say a word. He bent his head and kissed her. Which was perfectly fine with her. A happy Katie Summer reminded herself that there were other forms of communication. Wasn't she lucky that Jake was every bit as good at those as he was at conversation?

Philip Taylor Grant, Paige was discovering, was also good at conversation. When the ballroom became stuffy as it became crowded with people, he led Paige out onto the terrace. Music filtered out through the partially-opened French doors, and the chilly air felt refreshing. They sat on a stone bench, surrounded by other couples on other benches and chairs, and Philip talked about music.

"It's my great love," he said, and added apologetically, "I'm afraid I forget sometimes that everyone isn't as enchanted with the subject as I am. I hope I'm not boring you."

Paige laughed. She felt totally relaxed and very comfortable with this musician who, only hours earlier, she hadn't even known existed. "You'd have to talk about something other than music to bore me. Football, for instance, or calculus or the price of groceries or . . . well, almost anything but music."

Philip smiled. She had known, from the first minute she noticed him up on the stage, that he would smile exactly like that. And she felt a sharp pang because she had lied to him. Well, not exactly lied. Evaded the truth was more like it. Taking a leaf from Jake's book, she had said she was "taking a year off to think and plan my future." As she had known he would, he had assumed she meant taking a year off from college. When he asked what she was doing to fill her time, she'd answered casually, "Oh, I work on a newspaper."

"Oh? A daily?"

"No. A little weekly." No lie there. The school newspaper *was* published weekly.

Those meager answers on her part had seemed to satisfy him, at least for the time being. Paige, being a clever girl, quickly changed the subject to music again, specifically the evening's concert. And Philip had asked her no more personal questions.

"Well, hello there!" Virginia Mae's voice interrupted. "So this is where you've been hiding! We've been looking all over for you."

Paige's heart stopped at the sound of her stepmother's voice, but she quickly calmed down, reminding herself that her parents would hardly shout out her age for no reason. Still, the interruption annoyed her, and she remained seated, hoping they would go away.

They didn't. "Ah, I see you've found a friend."

Paige groaned silently. Wasn't it just like her father to talk to her in public as if she were playing in a sandbox? She stood up. "Mom, Dad, this is Philip Grant. Guest cellist with the Symphony." She said it proudly.

They acknowledged the introduction and complimented him on his performance. After a few moments of pleasant conversation, Virginia Mae said, "Paige, we really must head for home. It's getting quite late."

Paige did not want to hear that. But she knew that tone of voice. It meant there was no point in arguing. "Okay," she said reluctantly. "I'll meet you out front."

When they had gone, she turned to Philip. "I'd better get going. They don't like to be kept waiting."

He nodded. Putting his hand on her elbow, he led her back into the ballroom. In the entryway, he helped her with her blazer and then said, "Listen, I need your address. I'll pick you up about eight, how's that?"

"That's fine." She borrowed a piece of paper

and a pen from the hat-check girl and handed it to him.

He led her to the door. "Paige . . ." the expression on his face was serious, "I'm really glad you came tonight." He took one of her hands in both of his. "I thought this was going to be a dull evening. I was sure I wouldn't have anyone to talk to."

"It was fun for me, too," she said, smiling up at him. "I never know when I go somewhere with my parents if I'll have a good time or not." That should tell him she didn't *always* have chaperones when she went out, just in case he was wondering. "There's always a chance that there won't be anyone around under the age of forty."

He laughed. "Well, thanks for coming. I mean that. And I'll see you tomorrow night."

She almost said, "I can't wait," but bit her tongue just in time. Too childish. "I'll be ready at eight o'clock," she promised. And she turned and floated out the door and down the steps to her parents' waiting car.

CHAPTER 3

When Katie Summer awoke on Saturday morning, she was greeted by a sight that convinced her she was still asleep and dreaming. Paige was already up, and according to her bedside clock, it was only nine o'clock. But Paige was out of bed — on a Saturday morning. What's more, she was not only out of bed, she was standing in front of the full-length mirror wearing a formal gown of deep blue, tossing her head this way and that and muttering unhappily to her mirror image.

Katie sat up in bed. "Paige? What on earth are you doing?"

Caught by surprise, Paige whirled. "What does it look like I'm doing?" she snapped, cheeks flushing with annoyance coupled with embarrassment. "I'm trying on this stupid, ugly dress!"

Katie had to admit it wasn't the prettiest dress she'd ever seen. But then, she'd never particularly admired Paige's taste in clothing — too basic.

Sometimes even dull. But not this particular gown. It was so unlike Paige, Katie couldn't help staring at it. The puffed sleeves, stiff like huge paper flowers, the ruffles, thick and deep along the hem line, and those bows! Two at the waist and two on the bodice, like large blue growths! And it was all topped off by a full overskirt of stiff blue net. Katie shuddered. Had Paige actually *worn* that thing in public? And if she had, how had someone talked her into it?

"Miss Aggie," Paige said quietly, reading Katie's expression. She sank down on her bed, the ugly net overskirt sticking out stiffly around her. "It was Miss Aggie. Dad thought I should have an 'older woman' with me when I went shopping for a prom gown last spring." She shrugged. "This is what I took home from the store."

"Well, it's a gorgeous color on you. It just . . ." Katie struggled for the right words, "it just doesn't seem like your kind of dress. How did she talk you into it?"

Paige grimaced unhappily. "She was so busy with spring housecleaning, we didn't get out of the house to shop until five days before the prom. Everything fit to be worn in public was gone by then. This" — lifting the net disdainfully — "was the best of the lot, believe it or not."

Katie said soberly, "Boy, I would kill to see the rest of the batch!"

Paige laughed. At least Katie hadn't said the dress was beautiful or something equally stupid.

"Anyway," Katie continued, "if I'm not being too nosy, may I ask why you're trying it on at nine o'clock on a Saturday morning when as far as I know there's no big dance scheduled at school until the holidays?"

Paige brightened visibly. She got up and returned to the mirror. "*All* dances," she said smugly, "do not take place at Harrison High School. I," she announced, turning to face Katie, "am invited to a charity ball tonight, downtown at a major hotel. For *adults*." She raised her chin and spoke in a haughty voice, "All of the veddy best people will be there, my deah."

Katie giggled. "And you're wearing *that*?"

Paige crashed back to earth. "Oh, what am I going to do? I can't get a new dress today. Virginia Mae will never go along with that."

"Well," Katie said complacently, getting out of bed, "Ben should have given you more notice. When did he ask you, anyway?"

Paige laughed. "Katie, I'm not going with Ben!" Paige relished the wide-eyed stare that comment elicited.

"You're not? Who *are* you going with?"

Paige told her, describing Philip in glowing terms. "And how," she wailed as she finished, "can I meet him at the door in this dress? I look like Alice in Wonderland!"

She had neglected to mention Philip's age. So Katie had no reason to suspect that Virginia Mae would be anything less than cooperative. "Go ask Mom if you can get a new gown. I mean, the dance is for charity, right? And Mom's very big on charitable stuff. It can't hurt to try."

Paige looked grim. "The first thing she'll say is,

Why are you asking at the last minute? And the second thing she'll say is, That dress you have on is perfect." Taking another look in the mirror, she added, "But you're right. It's worth a try. What have I got to lose?"

"Why are you asking at the last-minute?" Virginia Mae, seated at the kitchen table going over the household accounts, wanted to know. In soft gray trousers and a light blue cashmere sweater, Paige thought her stepmother looked more like a college student than the parent of five children, three of whom were teenagers. With her blonde hair softly waving around her face, make-up discreetly applied to enhance her features, Virginia Mae was every bit as lovely, Paige thought, as any magazine model. But she didn't say that aloud. Her stepmother wasn't receptive to flattery, especially when it directly preceded a request.

"Absolutely not," came the answer to that request. "I haven't budgeted for a new gown this month," she said, holding up a handful of bills. "You know I need more warning than a few hours for a major expense. Besides," she turned back to her chore, "that dress you have on is perfect. And next time, tell Ben to give you more warning."

When Paige returned to the bedroom, Katie Summer looked up expectantly. She had dressed in jeans and a plaid blouse and was putting the finishing touches on her bed-making. "So? What did she say?"

Paige slammed the door and flounced over to her own bed. "Just exactly what I said she'd say."

She looked down at her gown in dismay. "Can you believe that anyone could think this dress was perfect for anything?"

Katie sat down opposite Paige. "C'mon, it's not that bad. What did Mom say when you told her you were going out with this . . . new person?"

Paige picked unhappily at the ruffles on her gown.

"Paige! You didn't tell her you're going out with someone new? Why not? We're always supposed to tell them who we're going somewhere with."

Sullenly Paige said, "She didn't ask. She was too busy explaining why it's absolutely necessary for me to go out of the house tonight looking like a wedding cake."

Katie laughed, not without sympathy. "Listen, I've got an idea. Come over here to the mirror. Where did I leave my scissors? Here they are, in the drawer. Now, come *on*. Trust me!"

Paige had remained perfectly still during Katie's brief monologue. She kept a wary eye on the scissors as she got up to follow her stepsister's instructions. "I don't object to this gown being sliced into rags if that's what you have in mind," she said, "but isn't that going to create a problem? I mean, I can't go to this ball in jeans and a crew-neck sweater, or sweats, or even a plaid skirt and blazer."

"Quit worrying," Katie assured her, "I know what I'm doing." On her knees, she busied herself with the hemline of Paige's blue gown. A ripping sound set Paige's teeth on edge.

"Katie! Are you *sure* you know what you're doing?"

"Trust me."

The last time Paige had trusted Katie had been when she was teaching Katie to drive. And she ended up in traction while Katie waltzed around the room in perfect health. But Paige would never say that aloud because she knew what a terrible time Katie had had working through her guilt from that accident, even though it wasn't Katie's fault.

As far as clothes were concerned, she had to admit that Katie Summer knew more about fashion than she did. If anything could be done about the monstrosity she was wearing, Katie could probably do it.

"Close your eyes," Katie ordered. "I don't want you to look until I've finished. Promise!"

"Oh, for Pete's sake, I promise. But just remember, as ugly as this thing is, it's still better than nothing. So take it easy, okay?" she said closing her eyes.

There were more ripping sounds and the snip-snip of scissors. Katie tugged and pulled and tore and snipped. Paige held her breath. When Katie finally said with satisfaction, "There! Now you can look," Paige was afraid to open her eyes.

"I can't look," she moaned.

"Sure you can," Katie contradicted cheerfully. "Go ahead!"

Paige opened her eyes and focused them on the mirror in front of her. "I don't believe it," she said slowly, her eyes widening. "What on earth did you do? You're a genius!"

Katie flushed with pleasure. "It's not bad, if I do say so myself."

Paige stared at her reflection. The ugly gown had, miraculously been replaced by a simple, full-length, electric blue sheath, fitted at the bodice, scooped at the neck. Gone were the puffed sleeves, the ruffles, the bows, and the net overskirt. Left were good, clean lines, a brilliant color, and elegant simplicity.

"A single strand of pearls, I think," Katie said, running to take the jewelry from the dresser and fasten it around Paige's throat. "You're lucky that taking all that junk off the dress didn't leave faded spots. You can't even tell there was anything there. I'll have to hem where I took off the sleeves, but that's all. What do you think?" But she already knew. The pleasure in Paige's face was self-evident.

"I think," Paige said sincerely, "that you've saved my life. Thank you, Katie."

Katie flushed with pleasure. This was a rare moment between them, and she couldn't help wishing they had more of them. Then she scolded herself mentally for being too greedy.

"Okay," she said, "so the problem of wardrobe is solved. But don't you have a few other problems?"

Paige tore her eyes away from the mirror. "Like what?"

Katie moved back to her bed and sat down.

"Didn't you have a date with Ben tonight, for instance?"

Paige's pleasure in her new gown disappeared. "Oh, that. Yeah, I guess I did. I'd better go call him."

"What are you going to tell him?"

Irritation spread across Paige's face. "It's not that big a deal, Katie. It was just a movie. People cancel dates all the time. Ben will understand."

"Are you going to tell him the truth? He's going to be really hurt, Paige."

Paige thought angrily, There she goes again, sounding like she's older than I am! "Whatever I tell him," she said sharply, "is between Ben and me and nobody else."

So much for the good moment between them.

But as Paige walked down the hall toward the telephone, she decided Katie was right. Ben *would* be hurt by the truth. So she didn't tell it to him. Not precisely. Instead, she told him something had "come up," and hoped he'd let it go at that.

He didn't. "Something came up? Like what kind of something?"

Paige sighed. She should have known. Ben was thinking about a future career in investigative reporting, because he loved asking questions and getting to the bottom of things. She should have known better than to tell someone like that that something had come up. She was going to have to tell an outright lie. It had all seemed so simple last night when she had accepted Philip's invitation. So innocent. Now it seemed much more complicated. She hated lying to Ben. He was so incredibly honest himself.

But, telling herself, a little lie was better than hurting him outright, she said, "A headache. I have this terrible headache. I just don't think I could sit through a movie."

There was a long moment of silence. Paige could easily visualize Ben's thin, earnest face concentrating on her words, sandy brows frowning over serious eyes behind horn-rimmed glasses. "Oh. Well, that's no problem. We don't have to see the movie. I can come over and we can just talk. I'll even make you some tea."

"I think I'll just sleep, Ben," Paige said. "I really would be rotten company." Paige, you are a terrible person, she scolded mentally. She was going to *have* to tell him the truth sometime, so she'd better pave the way right now. "If I feel better later, maybe I'll do something." She laughed, but it sounded hollow. "Hate to waste a perfectly good Saturday night." He didn't laugh. "But you go ahead and make other plans, Ben. I don't expect you to sit around waiting for my headache to go away."

"I don't mind," he said quietly.

"No, really, you go ahead. Talk to you later, Ben. 'Bye."

She felt terrible and argued with herself most of the afternoon. Ben would never do such a thing to her. And who *was* this Philip person, anyway? She hardly knew him. Ben, on the other hand, had been there for her. He'd seen her through some rough times during these first few months after the Guthrie clan descended upon the Whitman household. He'd made her feel attractive, even pretty, when everyone else was oohing and aahing over Katie Summer Guthrie. And, most important, he'd helped heal the bruise on her ego after Jake had gravitated toward Katie Summer. And Ben hadn't even known he'd done that, because he didn't even know that she'd hoped for something to develop between herself and Jake.

Didn't she *owe* him for all of that?

Several times that afternoon, Paige went to the telephone . . . to call Philip and cancel their date, then to call Ben and reinstate theirs.

But each time, she remembered her feelings of the night before: the sense of adventure and excitement and romance. And the thrill of having someone like Philip Grant single her — shy, awkward, unsophisticated Paige Whitman — out of that huge crowd. She just couldn't give up all of that.

"So, what did Ben say?" Katie asked when Paige returned from her phone call.

Paige shrugged. "No problem," she answered airily, and advanced toward the closet, wishing she could hide in there until Katie quit asking questions.

Katie's round blue eyes narrowed. "You told him the truth and that was okay with him?"

Paige didn't answer.

"You didn't *tell* him the truth, did you?"

Realizing Katie wasn't going to give up, Paige turned to face her. "No, I didn't. Not over the phone. But I *will*," she added hastily. "So you don't need to do it for me, in case that's what you're planning."

Katie looked genuinely shocked. "I wouldn't — "

"And you don't need to tell Jake, either. He might tell Ben. And Ben should hear it first from me."

"Yes," Katie said slowly, "he certainly should."

Paige's cheekbones flamed. "I said I will tell him. Why don't you just concentrate on your own life and stay out of mine?"

"Fine!" Katie snapped, getting up from the bed. "I'll do just that! Just don't ask me to lie for you, because that I won't do. You're on your own in this one." And she left the room, slamming the door behind her.

CHAPTER 4

Neither of Paige's parents had asked who her date for the evening might be. She realized they were assuming it was Ben and chose not to enlighten them. They'd find out for themselves soon enough — a moment she dreaded. Because Virginia Mae had, earlier that day, made a comment about Philip that heightened Paige's nervousness.

"That young man you were talking with last night," she had said after lunch, "seemed nice enough. I'm just sorry there was no one your own age at that party."

Paige didn't like the sound of that at all. Virginia Mae made Philip sound positively ancient. What was she going to say when he appeared in their living room that evening?

She'll probably ask him about his Social Security benefits, Paige thought dryly as she wound her long hair, shining from a twenty-minute shampoo, into a Grecian knot which she fastened at the back of her head. If she says one word about his age or mine in front of him, I'll never forgive her. I'll never speak to her again. I'll spend the rest of my high school years in total silence in this house. Then she relaxed, telling herself she was being silly. Virginia Mae was much too refined to say something, no matter *how* surprised she might be when Philip turned out to be her date instead of Ben.

Surprised was hardly the word. Total shock was more like it, Paige thought as she confronted her parents in the living room, with Philip at her side, looking splendid in his tuxedo. "Mom, Dad," she said in an astonishingly calm voice, "you remember Philip Grant? The cellist from the Symphony?" Mentioning music might help ease the stupified expression on her stepmother's face.

Paige's father extended his hand in greeting. "Nice to see you again. Drop by for any particular reason?" He was kidding, and Paige was delighted when Philip picked up on it. "Just out for a walk, sir."

"In your tuxedo?"

"Always wear it, sir," Philip responded with a straight face. "My mother used to tell me to be careful of the way I dressed when I went out, because one never knows when one might get hit by a car and have to be carted off to the hospital. I try to look my best at all times, thanks to her."

Virginia Mae finally opened her mouth. "Good evening, Mr. Grant," she said, her voice cool.

Paige's eyebrows went up. Her stepmother, she knew, wouldn't dream of addressing Ben as "Mr.

Collins." This was her way of emphasizing the silly little bit of difference in her's and Philip's ages. Honestly!

Virginia Mae's concentration switched from Philip to Paige's gown. Although her stepdaughter had wrapped a delicately hand-crochetted shawl around her shoulders, Virginia Mae wasn't fooled. "That isn't the gown you showed me today, is it? When did you go shopping?" Her tone of voice was deliberately casual, which told Paige her stepmother was really angry. But not, Paige was positive, about the dress.

"It's the same dress," she said, not looking at Virginia Mae. "Katie and I just made a few minor changes, that's all."

"I see. Well, you're both very clever. It's stunning." She didn't add, It's a bit sophisticated for someone your age, but Paige knew she was thinking it. She looked up and met her stepmother's eyes. They said quite clearly, This is not the end of this. I promise you, I will be waiting up when you walk through that front door later tonight, and we *will* discuss this then.

That was okay with Paige. The worst was over, for now. She was going out with Philip and no one was trying to stop her.

Tuck came downstairs just as Paige and Philip were leaving. She giggled softly to herself as she caught the expression on her stepbrother's face. He couldn't have looked more surprised, but he said nothing except, "Hi, there!" She knew he would corner her the first chance he got and ask her questions.

Smiling, she left the house with Philip. Their date was about to begin. And she was going to have a good time.

"A good time," she decided after an hour in Philip's company, was too tame a phrase. "A good time" was fine for a funny movie or a high school dance or a concert. But *this*, this evening full of fascinating conversation with Philip and his witty, sophisticated friends; of beautiful music to dance to; this evening of feeling as if she had somehow wandered accidentally into a new and exciting world, had to be called something more than just "a good time."

"Having a good time?" Philip asked, looking down at her as they whirled around the ballroom. High-ceilinged, with ornate molding topping the walls and trimming all doorways, the very size of the room dwarfed the crowd dancing there. Paige was thinking it would be a great place to hold a graduation ceremony. Or a football game.

She giggled. "I was just thinking that 'good time' didn't really cut it. Your friends are great! You must make friends quickly."

He shrugged. "Most of them are classical musicians. It doesn't take more than a few seconds to strike up a conversation with any of us. All anyone has to do is mention music."

"And this hotel," Paige continued, "is perfect, and the music is out of this world. No, I am not having a good time. I am having a fantastic time." She lowered her voice, afraid she'd gone overboard. Her lack of sophistication was showing. "Thank you for inviting me."

He smiled. "Thank you for coming. You're good company. I like your enthusiasm."

Was he saying he didn't mind her lack of polish? She felt so much younger than the other women in the room. Her cheeks felt hot. "I didn't mean to gush," she apologized. "I guess it's not cool to be so impressed, but I don't ordinarily move in these circles. I guess you already know that."

"One word I have absolutely no use for," Philip said sternly as the music stopped, "is the word *cool*. All it really means is a lack of emotion, and I don't approve of a lack of emotion. It makes no sense to me that it's considered 'uncool' to get very excited about something or to be very happy about something, or even to become angry about something. Sounds extremely boring to me. I've never understood what's so great about people hiding the way they feel."

Paige felt out of her depth. She wasn't sure if he was asking for her opinion or even if he expected her to *have* an opinion. The truth was, she'd never given the slightest thought to whether it was a good idea to be cool or not. She'd simply tried to be pretty much like everyone else around her. But now that Philip mentioned it, trying to be unemotional did seem pretty dumb.

He took her hand and led her over to the refreshment table. "Anyway," he added, looking into her eyes, "I'm glad you're not like that. Cool, I mean. You know how to have a good time and enjoy things, and I like that."

Paige was as surprised as he was impressed. In

her household, she wasn't the popular one. Katie Summer was. Paige had always preferred quiet things, like reading, and taking Scarlett for long walks in the park, and playing the piano. Parties really didn't interest her. Too much noise, too much mess, and too many people expecting her to sparkle. Katie sparkled with no effort at all, that was her personality. Paige had to work at it. But Philip was right. Last night, she'd had fun. And she was having fun tonight. Thanks to Philip.

And his friends. She couldn't believe the accepting way they responded to her. No one asked her her age or where she attended school. And since the bulk of every conversation centered around music, where Paige was on firm ground, she had no trouble relaxing completely. She laughed and talked and danced, and she felt beautiful and smart and clever, for the first time in her life.

"What are you doing tomorrow?" Philip asked as a dance ended.

She had just realized that the hands on the big clock out in the hall were inching dangerously close to one o'clock, her Saturday night curfew. Philip hadn't said a word about leaving. If he didn't mention it soon, another headache might become necessary.

His question interrupted her worrying. "Oh. I'm . . . I'm not doing anything special." She had planned to call Ben and tell him the truth, but maybe that could wait. It wasn't as if she was terribly anxious to explain about Philip. Ben had very high principles, and she knew that they didn't include fibbing. Okay, okay, *lying*.

"Great! Pick you up at two o'clock, okay? We'll find something to do. Is there a park anywhere near your house?"

"As a matter of fact, there's a park just down the hill from our house. I run Scarlett there."

"Scarlett?"

Paige laughed. "Our Irish setter. You missed out on the big thrill of having her jump up on you and lick you to death. She was out in the backyard when you arrived."

"I wouldn't have minded. I'm a dog-lover. If I didn't travel so much, I'd have one or two of my own."

Paige smiled at him. Of course he was a dog-lover. How could someone so nice *not* be?

She didn't want this evening to end. She didn't want to go home . . . *ever*. If only she lived alone, like Philip, and could come and go as she pleased! But remembering the look on Virginia Mae's face when she saw Paige's date for the evening, she knew it was absolutely crucial that she get home on time.

A young man appeared to tell Philip that they were all going out for pizza. Did Philip and Paige care to join them?

Paige stared at him. These people in their tuxedoes and evening gowns going for pizza? Paige found that funny, and almost giggled, until she realized sadly that she couldn't allow Philip to accept the invitation. If she had thought she would never see him again, she would have thrown caution to the winds and stayed out later. But Philip had already made a date with her for tomorrow. If she broke curfew, she'd be grounded. And how would she explain *that* to someone who thought she was as free as he was? And at least eighteen.

Philip turned to her for her opinion on the pizza.

"I'd really love to," she told him with a nervous smile. "But I've got this headache . . . two nights of dancing my feet off is catching up with me, I think."

"Oh, you're young and healthy," the young man protested. "You can take it."

She hoped fervently that he hadn't guessed just *how* young. Wasn't he staring at her in a funny way, like something about her wasn't quite right? Or was she imagining things because of her guilty conscience?

Philip rescued her. "Oh, hey, Paige, why didn't you say something? Of course you're tired. Listen, I'll take you home right now. I'm not hungry, really."

She thought he meant it. He seemed sincere. In the cab, she apologized for dragging him away from his friends.

He laughed and slid an arm around her shoulders. "Don't be silly. You should have said something about your headache sooner. I don't want you thinking I'm the sort of person who drags a girl out onto the dance floor when her head has clashing cymbals in it."

"I don't think that," Paige said, guilt washing over her like a cold rain. He felt bad about a headache she didn't even have.

Turning to face her on the back seat of the dimly-lit taxi, he said seriously, "Listen, are you sure you're going to be okay by tomorrow afternoon?"

Paige looked blank for a second. She'd been thinking about what she was going to tell Virginia Mae, who would surely be waiting up for her.

"The park, remember? You said you'd show me the park near your house. Or we could go to a museum if you'd rather. I understand Philadelphia has some great ones."

"I'd rather go to the park, if the weather's nice. Fresh air will take care of any leftover aches or pains." She grinned. "I think you should know that I throw a mean Frisbee. And Scarlett's a better catcher than any professional baseball player."

He looked happy. "You're sure?"

His dark hair was rumpled from the wind. It fell across his forehead haphazardly. His eyes on hers were intense, as if it really mattered what she answered. Oh, she was sure, all right. Even a real headache wouldn't have kept her from seeing him the next day.

When the taxi stopped in front of her house, Philip said quietly, "Just in case we don't have time up on the porch . . ." and pulled her against his chest to kiss her good night. Paige was surprised, but not so overwhelmed that she was unable to respond. He tasted of mint, and she smiled as they separated, thinking that he wasn't so sophisticated that he didn't worry about his breath when he kissed a girl. He really was the most considerate person she'd ever met.

"I'd better go in," she said, still smiling, and Philip nodded.

They were halfway up the steep steps when, to Paige's dismay, Jake's car pulled up behind the parked taxi and Katie Summer jumped out, laughing.

The last thing in the world she wanted was for Philip to meet Katie. If Jake was any example, older guys went for her stepsister. That was why Katie had Jake. Well, she wasn't getting Philip, too.

"Thanks for a lovely time," she said hurriedly as Katie started up the stairs. "See you tomorrow." And before Philip could argue, she turned and went inside. There will be no formal introduction to her stepsister *this* evening. If he asked her tomorrow who the blonde girl was, she'd say Katie was a student from Sweden that her stepmother had hired, to help look after Megan and Mary Emily and that she was leaving the country any day now.

Katie smiled at Philip as they passed on the steps, and said, "Hi!" He did the same and continued to his taxi.

Katie was impressed. He really was gorgeous, and the tuxedo didn't hurt. But wasn't Virginia Mae going to have something to say about Paige dating an older guy? She was pretty old-fashioned about things like that.

Paige came into the house, humming softly to herself, and found her stepmother waiting for her in the kitchen. She stopped short in the doorway and stopped humming. The expression on Virginia Mae's face sent her heart plummeting into her pumps. Paige heard the front door click shut. Katie. Her stepsister was about to be a witness to whatever lecture Virginia Mae had in mind. It was always such a treat to have an audience when you were being yelled at.

Virginia Mae stood up. Her oval face wore what Paige called her "mother look." It almost always preceded something Paige did *not* want to hear.

"Paige," her stepmother said as Katie Summer joined Paige in the doorway, "Philip Grant is too old for you. You are not to see him again."

CHAPTER 5

Paige's heart stopped when Virginia Mae announced that she could no longer see Philip Grant. She had been prepared for some arguing. But not for this. Not this arbitrary, laying-down-the-law, no-discussion statement that took her breath away. Not see Philip again? Charming, interesting, considerate, drop-dead-good-looks Philip?

No way!

In the doorway, Paige stared at Katie Summer, who had the decency to look embarrassed at being a bystander in this conversation. "I . . . I just wanted to ask Mom something."

"Ask! Then go away." Paige said irritably. She had no intention of giving in on this matter of seeing Philip again. She also had no intention of allowing her stepsister to sit in on the argument that was sure to come.

"Okay, okay! Mom, is the museum open tomorrow? Jake wants to go."

Virginia Mae was a part-time guide in a Philadelphia museum. She nodded.

"Okay if I go with him?"

"No homework?"

Katie shook her head. "I've finished all of it."

"All right then. Just make sure you're home by six for dinner."

Katie, avoiding Paige's eyes, told them both good night and left the kitchen.

Paige watched her go, a trace of envy in her dark eyes. How easy everything was for Katie Summer! She'd walked into a strange northern high school and quickly made friends, made the swim team, made things happen for herself. Then she'd wanted Jake — and she got him. No wonder she's bouncy and cheerful, Paige thought resentfully. Why shouldn't she be?

She turned to face her stepmother and saw with annoyed surprise that Virginia Mae was preparing to leave. She had rinsed her teacup at the sink and was reaching for the kitchen light switch.

"Wait a minute! You're not going to bed, are you?"

Virginia Mae's hand stopped in midair. "Of course I am. It's very late."

"You tell me I can't see Philip again, and then you go to bed?"

"He is too old for you, Paige," Virginia Mae said, keeping her voice low.

"He's only twenty-one. That's not old!"

"It's too old for a high school student. I'm sorry, Paige, but dating this young man is out of the question. And your father agrees with me, so you needn't tackle him first thing in the morning."

Paige was having trouble accepting what she saw as a drastic change in Virginia Mae. Someone had sneaked into the house and replaced her sweet, cheerful stepmother, with whom she got along so well, with this stern, no-nonsense authoritarian figure. She sounds just like Dad, Paige thought in dismay. One parent like that was more than enough!

She wasn't ready to give up. "Dad's four years older than you," Paige pointed out. She moved into the kitchen and leaned against the refrigerator, narrow chin held high. The kitchen was chilly, and she was freezing in the blue sleeveless dress and the thin shawl. But she knew if she ran upstairs to grab something warmer, there'd be no Virginia Mae in the kitchen when she returned.

"That's different."

Paige groaned aloud. Why did parents always say that? "What's different about it?"

"I'm not sixteen." Virginia Mae pulled her pink robe tightly around her. "I don't want to discuss this any more tonight, Paige. It's been a long day and I'm tired. We can talk about it more tomorrow if you insist." She faced Paige, her lovely face very serious. "But I warn you, your father and I won't change our minds. This matter is *not* negotiable. Turn off the lights when you come upstairs, please. Good night, dear."

Paige stood perfectly still in the chilly, empty kitchen. Don't call me dear, she thought, when you're telling me something I don't want to hear.

Paige loved her stepmother. The pretty, soft-spoken woman from Atlanta who shared Paige's enthusiasm for both music and the written word, had filled a very large hole in her life. And she had brought a new light into William Whitman's eyes after many years as a widower. Virginia Mae had tried to be a good mother to Paige and her ten-year-old sister, Megan. And she had made every attempt to be fair in conflicts between her stepchildren and her own children. Not that Megan had ever had anything beyond the most minor conflicts with ten-year-old Mary Emily Guthrie. Sharing a room was for them a real pleasure, because they genuinely liked each other. They had from the very first day the two families combined.

And Virginia Mae had never demanded special privileges for seventeen-year-old Tuck, even though he was the oldest of the five children.

And she had withstood, with remarkable forbearance, the almost-constant bickering of Paige and Katie Summer.

For all of that, Paige Elizabeth Whitman was deeply grateful.

But *none* of that, she decided as she switched off the light and left the kitchen, makes it okay for Virginia Mae to tell me I can't see a perfectly nice guy like Philip Grant. And as far as her father was concerned, well, it wasn't *her* fault he refused to accept the fact that she had grown up.

* * *

Katie was already asleep. Good. Paige didn't feel like answering questions about Philip. Shedding the dress, leaving it lying on the floor, a crumpled pool of bright blue, she slipped into pajamas and crawled into her unmade bed. Sleep would have to wait until she'd come up with a way to sidestep Virginia Mae's edict.

She couldn't say she was going to the park with Ben. He might very well show up at the house after she'd gone. He often dropped by on Sunday afternoon.

And if her parents remained immovable in their decision to end her relationship with Philip, he couldn't pick her up at home. They'd have to meet somewhere. Fortunately, he'd given her his telephone number.

But going to the park would be too risky. It was too close to the house. If her parents decided to take a Sunday afternoon stroll . . . Paige shuddered, visualizing the embarrassing confrontation.

She didn't want to lie to them. The best approach would be to use all of her powers of persuasion to change their minds. Philip *was* a nice person. They should at least give him a chance.

Satisfied with that plan and exhausted by two exciting evenings in a row, Paige fell asleep, feeling optimistic. She had convinced herself that there was still hope.

But she was wrong. That unpleasant discovery came at Sunday brunch. Her father was cheerfully cooking sausages and French toast when Paige came downstairs earlier than usual, anxious to have things settled.

"But it *is* settled," her father said when she stood beside him at the stove and asked if she could please talk to him about Philip. Miss Aggie had the day off, Tuck and Katie were reading the Sunday newspaper at the kitchen table, and Virginia Mae was playing the piano.

"He's too old for you and that's final," her father said. Then he flipped a slice of French toast, humming the song Virginia Mae was playing.

Paige was furious. What sort of person *hummed* as he ruined his daughter's life?

"You haven't even given him a chance!" Paige cried, forgetting to keep her voice low. Katie and Tuck glanced up from their newspaper sections. Paige tossed them a look that should have ripped the print right off the pages. They retreated to their reading. "He's a very nice person."

"I'm sure he is," her father said calmly, taking plates from the cupboard beside the stove. "That isn't the issue. You're sixteen; he's twenty-one. End of argument."

"That's *so* unfair!" She hated the fact that as he talked, he continued cooking, as if she were merely asking him if he thought it might rain this afternoon. This was *important*. And she had never liked French toast. "I promised to go to the park with him today." She stood up very straight, hands in her jeans pockets to hide their trembling. "I'm not going to call him up and tell him my parents won't let me go. I'd sound like a ten-year-old!"

He looked at her then. "You should have told us yesterday who was taking you to that ball. You deliberately let us think you were going with Ben. Which means you knew all along we wouldn't approve." He loaded a platter with steaming sausages and slapped it on the table. "So you can quit pretending to be surprised by our decision. You knew it was coming."

Well, yes. She'd suspected they'd have something to say about Philip's age. But she had thought she could convince them that age didn't matter.

Virginia Mae entered the room just then, and Paige decided to appeal to her stepmother's sense of propriety. Virginia Mae was the most polite person in the entire universe. "Just let me see him this afternoon," she begged. "It would be a lot more polite to tell him in person that I can't see him anymore. I know I shouldn't have said I could meet him without asking you first, and I'm sorry about that." She tried to look contrite but sensed that she hadn't succeeded. Her father looked skeptical. "It's just so *rude* to call someone on the telephone and cancel a date on such short notice." She was negotiating for time, and she knew it. If only they would let her keep this date, she would figure out later what her next move should be to keep Philip Grant in her life.

To her immense relief, Virginia Mae thought for a minute, exchanged a questioning glance with her husband, and then nodded. "All right. But this is the last time, Paige, and we expect you to make that perfectly clear to him. We will *not* change our minds about this."

Paige heaved a sigh of relief. She had the time she'd hoped for. She'd think of something to keep this relationship going. "Oh, thanks, both of you," she gushed, even as she noticed Katie giving her a glance loaded with suspicion. Ignoring it, Paige added seriously, "This really *is* the most polite way to do things. Now, if I could please be excused, I'm really not hungry. And I want to clean my room."

Katie choked on her sausage.

Giving her a baleful look and receiving permission from Virginia Mae to skip brunch, Paige escaped. When Philip arrived, she wanted to be completely ready to leave. Any time he spent in the company of her parents was dangerous. She couldn't risk having them comment on the age difference. It would be just like Virginia Mae to mention that she was sure he understood their feelings. Then Philip would want to know what she was talking about. And Virginia Mae just might mention Paige's birth date. Horrors!

She needn't have worried. Ten minutes before Philip was due to arrive, her parents left the house with Megan and Mary Emily to go for a drive in the country.

"Remember, Paige," Virginia Mae said as they were leaving, "our decision about Philip Grant is final. See that you make that clear to him."

"Right." Now please leave, Paige urged mentally.

They left.

Philip arrived just minutes after the station wagon pulled away. He looked different. Contrary to the joking comment he had made to her father the night before, he was not wearing a tuxedo. He was dressed, instead, in jeans, sneakers, and a white sweatshirt with the word, JULLIARD printed on the front. He looked absolutely wonderful, and her heart jumped, taking her by surprise. She hadn't expected his appearance to knock her entire system for a loop like that. She'd only known him for two days. And she'd never been the kind of person who went all mushy because of a male person. That was more Katie's kind of thing. But now . . . that slightly off-center smile, those penetrating but warm eyes. . . .

"You went to Julliard in New York City?" she asked.

He nodded as they went down the steps. "Yeah," he said with a grin, "and if I'd known that you were just a hop, skip, and a jump away in Philly, I'd have spent most of my spare cash on train fare."

No one had ever said anything like that to her . . . or made her feel so important. Well, her father had a long time ago. She had acted as hostess for him more than once at parties he'd given for his friends. And, at his urging, she had entertained at the piano for his guests. He had been generous with his thanks and his praise. But now, someone else was his hostess, someone else played Chopin at their parties.

Think, Paige, think! she ordered mentally,

pointing out the way to the park. Think of a way to keep this person in your life. Everyone else in the family has someone. Mom and Dad are still on their honeymoon, most of the time. Megan and Mary Emily have each other. Katie Summer has Jake and Tuck sort of has Jennifer Bailey. It's not fair that you can't have Philip.

Ignoring the little voice that argued, Ah, but you *do* have someone, Paige, you have Ben, she called out as they reached the bottom of the stairs, "C'mon, I'll race you to the park! Last one there is a rotten egg!"

Laughing, Philip accepted the challenge and took off across the street, dark hair blowing across his forehead.

Paige was right beside him.

CHAPTER 6

Strolling up to the Rodin museum, Jake's hand in hers, Katie spied a familiar figure just ahead of them, viewing the sculptor's most famous work of art. It was Ben Collins, as lost in thought as the figure depicted in front of him. Katie tugged at Jake's hand, intent on steering him in a different direction to avoid questions about Paige, but before Jake could respond, Ben glanced up.

"Hey, you two!" he called. "C'mere!"

Katie hesitated. She didn't want to talk to Ben. Suppose he asked her about Paige? What was she supposed to say? Still, he was a friend and couldn't be ignored. They would have to say hello.

It struck her, as they joined Ben, that he had a lot in common with the statue that held his interest. Ben was a thinker, too.

"No matter how many times I see this," Ben said quietly, "I never get tired of it."

"I was just thinking that it reminded me of you," Katie commented. "I've seen you sitting just like that on campus, more than once. With your elbow on your knee, your head resting on your hand."

"Ever wonder," Jake asked, "what this guy is puzzling over? World peace, maybe? A decent minimum wage? The Army-Navy game?"

"No question," Ben answered casually. "Women."

Katie laughed nervously, while Jake nodded agreement. "Yeah, you're right. Makes you wonder if he ever figured them out, doesn't it?"

"No," Ben said, "I'm convinced he never did. How could he?" Turning to Katie, he asked the question she'd been dreading. "How's Paige? Her headache gone?"

So, Paige still hadn't told him the truth. Katie was not about to do that *for* her. "I guess so."

"Good. Maybe I'll drop in on her when I finish here."

Katie hesitated. It would be a really rotten thing for Ben to discover Paige in the park with Philip. Someone should warn him. On the other hand, Virginia Mae had made it clear to Paige that she was to tell Philip good-bye and then come back home. Probably, Paige had already done that and was home hoping Ben would drop by.

Then, remembering the look in Paige's eyes when she left the bedroom that morning, Katie admitted to herself reluctantly that Paige would give up Philip when grass was purple and not a minute sooner.

"She might not be home," she said. "I think she said she had errands to run." She hoped the guilt she was feeling wasn't registering on her face. She wasn't a very good liar.

"Errands on Sunday?"

"The drugstore in our neighborhood is open. Maybe she had to go there."

"Well, I think I'll take my chances. See you guys later." Ben went off into the museum, his shoulders slightly hunched, his steps hurried, as always.

"That guy needs to learn to relax," Jake said amiably. "He always looks like he's carrying all of the problems of this planet on his shoulders."

Katie nodded grimly. "Yeah. And the last thing he needs right now is another problem."

"Like what?"

"Never mind. Let's go in. C'mon!" She tugged at his hand. She wasn't ready yet to tell him what was going on at home. If he thought her parents were being unfair and said so, they'd probably argue, and she didn't want that.

She could only hope that if Ben got to their house and found Paige still absent, he wouldn't decide to take a solitary walk in the park. Telling herself that Paige was probably safely home now, Katie made up her mind to concentrate on the museum's exhibits. Paige was perfectly capable of making her own choices.

Katie was right in her estimation of Paige's ability to make choices. But Paige was having more trouble with the choice at hand than she'd ever had before. Sitting on a rock deep in a heavily wooded area of the park, listening to Philip talk about a particular piece of music he was struggling with, she knew there was simply no way she could follow her parents' order. Not see him again? This sensitive, witty, intelligent person. Not get to know him better? Cut him out of her life because he was a puny five years older than she was? She wasn't going to do it.

But that meant a mega-major defiance of a direct order from her parents. Deciding she was going to continue seeing Philip was one thing. Figuring out the details was something else. Those details, she knew, had to include lying. Lying to her family, lying to Philip. He could never pick her up at the house again, or even come to the park with her. If she decided to go on seeing him, she'd have to meet him somewhere away from the house. And what excuse would she give him? And what would she tell her parents?

She needed more time to think this through. It wasn't fair that she didn't have it.

Lost in angry thought, she didn't hear Philip when he said, "Penny for your thoughts." He had to repeat it.

"Oh, I'm sorry," Paige apologized. "I guess I was daydreaming." They were sitting close together on a huge boulder, knees drawn up, arms clasping legs. It was a beautiful day, the few leaves left above them radiating autumn colors of scarlet, red, and orange, the sun warming their faces. The wooded area they had gravitated toward was unoccupied except for a host of squirrels scurrying about. Paige felt safe and happy and wanted to stay there forever.

"Come hear me play Wednesday night? I'll feed you afterward, as a reward."

Paige thought frantically. No problem getting out of the house; she'd think of something. Bus stop two blocks away to take her downtown. Take the same bus home, get in by eleven. . . . "Sure. I'd love to. What's the program?"

While he told her, her brain worked out the details. A weeknight concert should be over by ten. Could they eat in forty-five minutes? Her heart sank. Even if they did, the bus ride alone took thirty minutes.

"My last piece is midway through the program," Philip said, "so I can probably get away then."

Paige smiled, relief warming her like the sun above them. They'd have plenty of time if Philip left the stage early. Piece of cake.

"But if you'd prefer to stay for the complete performance, I can join you in the audience."

"No, I think I'd rather leave when you're finished. That will give us . . ." she stopped, her cheeks flushing scarlet.

". . . More time together," he finished, matching her smile. Then he put an arm around her shoulders, pulled her close and sealed their agreement to meet on Wednesday night with a kiss. Paige's response was tinged with anger toward her parents. They're just not being fair!

It seemed to her that anything she did would be justified by that unfairness. She wouldn't have to lie if they would be more understanding. There wouldn't have to *be* any deception if they would just give Philip a chance.

Over Philip's sweatshirted shoulder, she spied a lone figure some distance away, running across the park. There was no mistaking that bony frame, those slumped shoulders. It was Ben. He couldn't see them because of the woods, but she could see him quite clearly. He looked . . . so alone. Or was her imagination just being fired by her guilt? Had he stopped at the house to see her? Had he come to the park looking for her? He didn't seem to be searching. His head was down, and he wasn't looking around.

I have to tell him, she thought clearly. I have to tell him *something*.

But if she told him the truth, he might tell Katie. Yet Katie wouldn't fink on her unless the two of them had a fight. But they had so many fights. . . .

As the sun vanished behind thickening clouds, Philip said he would walk her home and catch a bus.

That seemed safe enough. Nothing to hide right now. Her parents knew she was with Philip . . . *this* time. Paige wished with everything in her that it could continue like this. If only she could go on seeing Philip, with her parents' approval. But there was no chance of that.

She could only hope Philip wouldn't kiss her

again in front of the house. Anybody could be watching from a window.

He didn't. And she went inside feeling conflicting emotions. She was glad she was seeing him Wednesday night, upset that she couldn't see him openly, and guilty about Ben.

She was cool to everyone at dinner, except Megan and Mary Emily, who didn't know what was going on. She answered in monosyllables any question directed her way by her parents, and kept her eyes on her plate. Conversation flowed around her, but she took no part in it, and she left the table the second she had swallowed the last of her meal.

She was lying on her bed, daydreaming about Philip, when a knock sounded on the bedroom door. Katie was in the bathroom and Paige made a face of annoyance, not wanting her precious private time interrupted. But the knock, when it came again, was insistent.

"Oh, come in!" she said, sitting up.

Virginia Mae entered the room. Paige's face instantly became expressionless. She knew the forthcoming discussion would be about Philip. But short of jumping out the bedroom window, she couldn't avoid talking to her stepmother.

"Paige," Virginia Mae said in her soft Georgian drawl, "I know you're angry right now. But your father and I are only thinking about what's best for you. We're not trying to be cruel."

What's best for me is Philip, Paige thought.

"This young man is twenty-one years old. He

lives on his own. He travels. He no longer requires parental supervision."

Parental supervision? That sounded suspiciously like legalese. Virginia Mae had probably borrowed that one from her lawyer-husband.

"But none of those things is true for you. So you couldn't really have all that much in common with him. Does he know how old you are?"

Paige ignored the last question. "It's not true that we have nothing in common," she said quietly. "He makes me laugh. He listens when I talk. He thinks I'm pretty, and he likes my enthusiasm. And we both love music. We talk about it all the time." And when he kisses me, Paige thought, I feel beautiful and smart and kind, and nothing else ever made me feel that way. What we have in common is that we feel good together. How can that be wrong?

Virginia Mae reached out and patted Paige's hand.

Paige snatched it away as if the gentle touch had scalded her. She didn't need to be treated like the family pet.

Her stepmother frowned, and sighed, and smoothed her blue skirt self-consciously.

I'm sorry, Paige thought. I didn't mean to hurt your feelings. But the words never made it to her mouth.

Virginia Mae stood up. "I guess you need more time. I do hope you'll work at understanding this, Paige. I would feel terrible if you let this come between us, and I know your dad would, too."

At the doorway, Virginia Mae hesitated. "Ben stopped by this afternoon. He seemed disappointed that you weren't home. I said I would have you call him."

"What did you tell him I was doing?"

"Why, I just said you were out, that's all. Anything else will have to come from you, Paige." She hesitated in the doorway. "I do think you should call him. He seemed . . . puzzled. I think he deserves some sort of explanation."

I don't *want* to talk to Ben, Paige thought.

Virginia Mae left, concern in her face.

I am going to drown in guilt, Paige thought as she lay back down and rolled over on her side, her back to anyone entering the room. Biting her lower lip in frustration, she decided she wouldn't *let* herself drown. Besides, she had a life preserver, didn't she? She had Philip.

She heard the door open and knew it was Katie. The flowery cologne was a dead giveaway. Paige remained stationary.

"Paige, are you asleep?"

Go away, Paige thought fiercely.

"We ran into Ben at the museum today. He asked about your headache. Don't you think now that you can't see Philip anymore, you should call Ben? He doesn't understand what's been going on."

"Don't worry about Ben, Katie. You just worry about Jake and leave Ben to me."

Katie wasn't quite ready to give up. "Ben is *my friend*, too, Paige. He was very nice to me after the accident. And it's embarrassing and awkward when I know something about you that he doesn't know. That's not fair to Ben *or* to me."

Paige flipped over angrily. "Who ever told you the world was fair? Not *me*, that's for sure!"

Katie gave up. Ben would just have to take care of his own problems.

She hoped, for the sake of the entire family, that Paige had taken care of hers.

But she wasn't at all convinced that Paige had.

CHAPTER 7

At school on Monday, Paige avoided Ben all day. But she couldn't avoid the journalism office when classes were through for the day. She had assignments waiting for her. Ben would probably forgive her dating someone else faster than he would her failure to hand in an article by deadline.

"Hi," she said casually as she entered the room noisy with clacking typewriters. He had obviously been waiting for her, standing just inside the door instead of sitting at his desk or arguing with Laurie, his coeditor. "What's up?"

"How's your headache?" He said it with innocent concern, which told her that he hadn't heard a word from Katie Summer. Good. She would tell him herself. But not now, of course, not here. Later.

"Oh, it's gone now." She moved toward the file cabinets at the back of the room. He followed.

She found herself wondering what he would look like in a tuxedo. But her imagination failed her. Ben just wasn't the tuxedo type. He was the flannel shirt or sweater and jeans type.

"I called Saturday night," he said quietly as she leafed through a sheaf of file folders. "Megan said you went out. I guess you felt better."

She shrugged. "I needed some fresh air. I hope you didn't stay home all night. I told you not to."

"Couldn't find anyone to see the film with. I hit the books instead. Where were you yesterday afternoon?"

The question caught her off-guard. "Oh. I . . . I went out for a little while."

"Alone?"

She knew she should look at him, but she couldn't. "Um . . . no, with a friend. Mom said you stopped by. Sorry I wasn't home." This was a lot harder than she had thought it would be. He was asking too many questions.

She was rescued by Laurie, who called out to Ben that he was desperately needed.

"Just a minute."

"No! Now! This second! This can't wait. Get over here!"

"Paige. . . ."

She turned then, to look up at him and was stunned by the pain in his eyes. He knows, she thought with clarity, and he's worried.

"Ben!"

"Coming. Talk to you later?" he asked Paige.

"Sure. Later." And thought to herself, This is

awful. He's worried about us and all I can think about is Philip. How on earth am I going to handle this?

She handled it that particular day by not talking to Ben later. When she had finished her assignments, she waited until Ben was deep in a heated discussion with Laurie and then slipped out of the room and went home. After dinner she talked Katie into going to the branch library with her. That way, she wouldn't be home if Ben called.

"Ben called," Virginia Mae announced when her daughters returned home later that night. "He wants you to call him back."

But Paige didn't. She knew she couldn't avoid answering Ben's questions indefinitely. Not only was it a rotten way to handle things, it just wasn't possible. She had no intention of giving up the newspaper and Ben *was* a coeditor. If she wanted to continue her newspaper work, she would have to straighten things out with him. But how?

The truth? "Ben, I'm sorry, but I've found someone I like better?" That was cruel. He'd be hurt. Wouldn't he? Most people thought Ben was invincible, that nothing touched him deeply. He seemed so in control. But she knew better. Anyone who could be as gentle and sweet as Ben was in their private moments together, felt things deeply.

But she couldn't keep lying to him. He was too smart to fall for that.

The problem seemed insoluble. So Paige did what she often did when she was tired of wrestling with a problem: She put it aside. Maybe it would solve itself. Maybe Ben would meet a gorgeous new student tomorrow and fall madly in love. He'd come to Paige and say sadly, "Gee, Paige, I feel awful about this, but I just can't help it. I hope you'll forgive me."

And she, being a generous person, would forgive him with a sweet smile, saying they would always be friends. And then she'd be off the hook, free to enjoy her relationship with Philip.

As long as you're daydreaming, an inner voice said dryly, how about fantasizing away your parents' objections to Philip?

But that was too monumental a stumbling-block even for an imagination as fertile as hers.

She thought about asking Katie Summer for advice. Katie seemed to have an inborn knack with guys. She had certainly zapped Jake away fast enough, with little more than a fluttering of her eyelashes and that dazzling smile of hers.

On second thought, she wouldn't go to Katie. Katie was, after all, Virginia Mae's daughter. And hadn't she said on the way home from the library the other night, "You really should talk to Mom about Philip. Try to make her understand how you feel. Maybe you could change her mind."

Paige had argued that she'd tried, to no avail. "Your mother isn't famous for changing her mind," she'd said. Katie had responded defensively that it all depended upon how arguments were presented to Virginia Mae, making it sound like the disagreement was all Paige's fault.

Deciding against turning to her stepsister,

Paige pushed the entire matter of Ben and Philip and her parents out of her head. She was seeing Philip Wednesday night. She would concentrate solely on that for now. Everything else would just have to wait.

Ben waited by the telephone all evening. He went to bed promising himself he'd be patient with Paige, although he was not by nature a patient person. But Paige was important to him. Whatever was going on with her, he wasn't going to push. Backing her into a corner would just make her quills stand on end. And he didn't want to blow the relationship by forcing an issue when he didn't even know what the issue was. Another guy? Maybe. But who? If she'd met someone at school, he'd have heard about it. Gossip flourished at Harrison like fungus in a rain forest. Katie might not tell him, out of loyalty to Paige, but someone else would have.

But if it wasn't another guy, what *was* it? Why had Paige suddenly turned cool? Family problems? He knew she wasn't all that happy at home these days. But she'd seemed comfortable talking to him about the situation there and had never turned silent on him in the past. Why was she avoiding him, not returning his phone calls? And where had she been all weekend?

He would have to wait until she felt like answering those questions. It wouldn't be easy.

"I've got a field trip tomorrow night," Paige announced at breakfast on Tuesday morning. She stirred the cereal in her bowl, avoiding direct contact with the inquiring eyes of either parent. "We're meeting at school at seven." That would give her plenty of time to take the bus downtown. "I'm not sure what time I'll be home. Maybe late."

"And you're going where?" her father asked.

"Offices of the *Chronicle*". It was a weekly newspaper with mostly ads. Her father never bothered with it.

"Why visit there at night?" he continued. "Seems to me you'd learn more when there is activity there."

"Oh, but that's the point," she said quickly. "It's a weekly, comes out every Thursday morning, so Wednesday night is when they put the paper to bed. That's the most exciting time. We'll learn more than we would during the day."

"I don't remember seeing a permission slip," Virginia Mae said.

Paige felt Katie's eyes on her face. Mind your own business, she telegraphed mentally. "It's here somewhere. Probably lurking in the depths of my purse. I'll dig it out before tomorrow."

"Fine." Virginia Mae nodded and turned her attentions to Megan and Mary Emily, who were begging to take Scarlett to school with them. "Don't be silly. Dogs are *not* allowed in school, and you both know it."

Paige took advantage of the shift in attention and left. Walking to school alone, scuffing her booted feet through fallen leaves on the sidewalk, she was daydreaming about Philip when she heard her name called. Turning, annoyance filled her as Katie ran to catch up with her. She didn't feel like company. And she especially didn't feel like answering any of Katie Summer's questions. She had been deliberately vague during their discussions to and from the library, but she couldn't keep that up forever. Sooner or later, Katie would ask her if she'd told Philip she couldn't see him anymore.

"So, did you tell Philip you couldn't see him anymore?" were the first breathless words out of her stepsister's mouth. "What did he say? Was he hurt? Angry? What?"

I will give the truth to the six o'clock news team before I'll give it to her, Paige thought firmly. "Don't I always do as I'm told?" she asked lightly.

Katie thought for a minute. Then, as they crossed the street, she answered honestly, "No. Not always. You're not a saint, Paige."

"Oh, and I suppose you are."

"No, of course not. I just meant . . ."

Paige spotted Judy Belnap, her best friend, walking up ahead. "I have to ask Judy about something. See you later." And she ran after Judy, calling out to her.

If Paige Whitman told Philip Grant good-bye, Katie thought grimly, I'll eat my swim medals. She's too cheerful. If she'd done what Mom and Dad said, she'd be moping around like a dying flower.

Thinking of what a major disruption would do to an already-shaky family, Katie shivered. They were just now putting that horrid automoblie accident behind them. Was this defiance about Philip Paige's way of making up for the horrors she'd suffered: the injury to her leg, the excrutiatingly painful recovery, the isolation she'd felt, unable to live a normal life?

Or was Paige simply so taken with Philip that she couldn't help herself?

Katie groaned. Do we always have to go from one crisis to another? Can't we Whitmans and Guthries ever be normal and boring, just for a little while?

It never occured to her that perhaps, for a combined family of seven people, their life *was* normal.

When she reached school and met her friends, she put Paige's situation out of her mind. Sara asked, "Why so glum, chum? You look like you lost your best friend, and I know you didn't, 'cause I'm standing right here." Katie managed a weak smile. She had already made up her mind that she would *not* check the front hall bulletin board to see if there really was a field trip to the *Chronicle* scheduled on Wednesday evening.

"Let's check out the bulletin board," Diane said, dragging Lisa, Sara, and Katie toward the huge cork board in the front hall.

Well, it's not *my* fault, Katie told herself as she scanned the board for any field trips slotted for Wednesday. Diane made me look. She was not surprised to see that there were no field trips at all on Wednesday.

So. Not only had Paige not told Philip goodbye, she was seeing him Wednesday night.

"Katie! I've asked you three times if you finished your English essay," Sara scolded. "Quit daydreaming and come back to earth."

"Sorry. Yes, I finished it."

But she didn't tell her friends what she had been thinking about. If Paige was determined to pursue this relationship with Philip, that was her business.

But it was their parents' business, too, and there was no question in Katie's mind that they'd find out. When that happened, she wanted to be on a plane headed for anywhere. She did not want to be home. Deliberate defiance of a direct order would make everything else that had happened to the Whitman-Guthrie clan seem as trivial as spilling a glass of milk at the dinner table. *This* defiance was major.

Oh, Paige, Katie thought, please don't do this!

Paige did it, anyway. Wednesday evening, claiming innocently that she had lost the elusive permission slip, she left the house after dinner to take the mythical field trip. Virginia Mae wasn't all that happy about the missing form, but she didn't argue when Paige said, "Most of the kids don't even bother with them, Mom. The teachers never collect them."

Swallowing her guilt, Paige left the house by the front door and proceeded directly to the garage, where she slipped quietly in the side door and collected the black velvet skirt she had hung there earlier in the day. Then she ran down the hill and across the street to a gas station rest room, locking the door. The large shoulder bag she carried everywhere with her contained extra makeup, clips to hold her long, straight hair high on her head, even a pair of pumps, and a small clutch bag. She slipped out of her jeans, stashed them in a crumpled roll behind the toilet tank, and slid the skirt over her white silk blouse. Makeup and hair to transform her appearance from that of a sixteen-year-old school girl to someone older took longer than she'd expected. Her fingers were shaking with nervous tension as she hid the shoulder bag behind a large brown plastic wastebasket and left the rest room.

The entire deception, she thought as she waited for the bus, had almost been thrown right out the window that afternoon when she'd run into Miss Aggie as she was heading for the garage with the skirt.

"Where are you going with that skirt?" the housekeeper had asked.

"Oh." She'd been so sure everyone was too busy to notice what she was doing. She'd forgotten about Miss Aggie. "There were people smoking at the party after the concert the other night. This skirt smells like an ashtray. I'm just going to air it out."

Miss Aggie looked skeptical. "In the garage?"

"Well, it looks like rain, and I might forget it's outside. Rain would ruin it. Besides, I'll just open the garage door and let some air in."

It had been a close call. Virginia Mae never would have bought that story. But Miss Aggie had. Or if she hadn't, she'd pretended to.

Any guilt Paige felt over her deception vanished the minute she saw Philip waiting for her outside the concert hall. It struck her as amazing that a person could look equally wonderful in a tuxedo or in jeans and sweatshirt.

"I thought you might like to watch from backstage," he said after telling her how glad he was that she could come. "I have permission for you to do just that, if you'd like. And I also have permission to leave after the rococo theme, so we'll have more time."

Paige smiled happily. Everything was working out beautifully.

Which must mean that she was doing the right thing.

Wasn't she?

CHAPTER 8

It was exciting being backstage. Paige watched the hustle and bustle with wide eyes, sorry that she couldn't share what she was experiencing with her parents when she got home. Virginia Mae, especially, would be fascinated.

She was also thinking that she could have worn jeans and no one would have cared. She could have saved herself the trouble of hiding her clothing at the gas station. What if her jeans were gone when she got back there? She could hardly walk into the house after a field trip, wearing a long black velvet skirt.

"Well? Philip asked eagerly when he led her from the hall some ninety minutes later. "What did you think? Have a good time back there?"

"It was great! I never realized how much work it took to get a group of musicians on stage."

It was a clear, crisp night, the stars lighting the sky above them. "Feel like walking?" Philip asked. "There's a great diner just up the street. Very ordinary, but the food is great."

Paige glanced at her watch. They had plenty of time. "Sure! I'd love to walk. Let's go!"

He was right about the food. It was delicious. And the diner, almost empty, was quiet and warm and cozy. They sat opposite each other on blue vinyl seats in a booth. The smell of roast beef and grilled sandwiches mixed with the sounds of country music from a radio hidden somewhere in the kitchen as Paige and Philip discussed the concert.

She loved his eyes. So dark they were almost black, they should have seemed cold, she thought, like lumps of coal. Instead, little specks of gold and brown warmed them as Philip leaned forward to take her hands in his. She thought of the hot chestnuts sold on street corners in New York City. She had always loved them, and had chosen them many times over a hot dog or soft pretzel.

"Ever travel much?" he asked her. The waitress had cleared their plates away and taken their dessert order.

Paige shook her head. "Not really. We've gone to New York a lot, but that's certainly not much of a trip." She didn't mention the trip to Atlanta for her father's wedding. She was sure that by travel Philip wasn't referring to a station wagon crowded with five cranky children, whose single parents had just turned their familiar worlds upside-down by becoming a couple.

"Traveling has its drawbacks," he said, "but it's an education. It's a great way to learn about people. And," smiling, "there are fringe benefits sometimes."

Paige laughed. "You mean the food in this diner?"

"Right. The food in this diner." Philip looked directly into her eyes as the waitress left after depositing two servings of apple pie with vanilla ice cream. "Among other things."

Paige wished desperately that she could seize this moment and hold onto it. This had to be one of the best nights of her life, and she wasn't even supposed to be here. If her parents had their way, she'd have no more moments like this one.

It wasn't fair.

They walked, hand-in-hand, back to the concert hall, where Paige would catch her bus home. Philip had offered to ride with her, but she told him that was silly. He'd just have to turn around and ride all the way back alone. Privately, she was thinking that you never could tell who might be on that bus. A neighbor could see her sitting there with Philip and just casually mention to Virginia Mae the next day, "My, isn't that a nice-looking young man Paige is seeing now?" That, she didn't need!

"Saturday afternoon" Philip said, "there's a party. Go with me?"

She knew he was working Saturday night. Which meant they would leave the party by seven.

"I'd love to go. I'll be downtown shopping Saturday afternoon, so why don't I just meet you here at four o'clock?" That way, she could leave the house any time she wanted to and fill in the hours until the party somehow. Perhaps go to the library? Maybe.

The streetlights above them bathed his face in a soft glow. "Okay. Come on inside when you get here and go backstage. Harry, the guy at the door, knows who you are now. I'll tell him you're coming. He'll let you in. I don't want you stuck out here in the cold."

Perfect. She could leave the house at a normal hour and come straight here. Virginia Mae would have no reason to ask questions.

The concert had ended, and people were beginning to stream from the hall.

"Quick!" Philip said, pulling Paige toward him, "kiss me before we're surrounded."

Paige had no problem with that request.

"I'll call you," he promised as her bus pulled up to the curb. "Tomorrow night."

She nodded and turned away. And found herself staring at Katie Summer. Jake, in a suit and tie, was with Katie.

Assuming immediately that her stepsister was spying on her, Paige blurted rudely, "What are *you* doing here?"

Katie, looking lovely in a powder blue coat, could just as easily have asked, *This* is your field trip? But she didn't. "What everyone else is doing here. We went to the concert." Attempting a small laugh, she added, "This is our week for culture, I guess. Sunday the museum; tonight the Symphony."

Paige wondered if Katie had seen the kiss. Probably. The last place in the world she would ever expect to run into Katie was at a classical music concert. And weren't those big, blue eyes just chock-full of disapproval? Running into her like this was a major complication.

"Philip, this is my stepsister, Katie Summer Guthrie and Jake Carson."

Philip said hi to Katie and shook hands with a friendly Jake. Paige wondered how much, if anything, Katie had told Jake about Philip. Her mind raced frantically. She could hardly warn Katie, in front of Philip, not to say anything at home about running into Paige. Besides, Katie knew perfectly well that Paige was defying their parents. She wouldn't tell, would she? Maybe not out of loyalty to Paige, but because she absolutely loathed family problems.

To her relief, neither Katie nor Jake had noticed that she was about to board a bus. They simply assumed that Philip was taking her home. Good. Because how could she refuse if they offered her a ride home? Yet, she couldn't have accepted. She had to stop at the gas station and retrieve her things and change her clothes and hair.

Conscious of the bus making impatient noises, she did nothing to encourage conversation with Katie and Jake. Taking the hint, Katie said, "Well, we'd better get going. See you later," and led Jake away. Paige ignored the dubious glance Katie tossed over her shoulder as they left. She'd deal with that later.

She waited for Philip to say, "Wow! That's your sister? She's really beautiful, isn't she?"

He didn't say that. Instead, he said, "So that's your stepsister. I passed her on your steps the other night. She's awfully young, isn't she? I guess it would be more fun for you if she was closer to your age. Just a high school kid, isn't she?"

Paige's toes curled in her pumps. Katie Summer was only one year younger than *she* was.

While she was grateful that Philip hadn't been impressed by Katie's looks, that gratitude was cancelled out by his casual dismissal of Katie as "just a high school kid." So she'd been right all along, not telling him her age. She had thought the age difference mattered only to her parents, but maybe it wasn't as trivial as she'd thought. It sounded like Philip might very well feel the same way about it that Virginia Mae did.

Her bus was making sounds indicating a momentary departure. She thanked Philip again, he promised once more to call her, and she got on the bus. Making her way to the back, she took the only vacant window seat. Spotting her there, Philip grinned and saluted. She thought he looked like a magazine cover or a movie ad. She was glad Katie Summer had run into them, even though it could mean trouble. Maybe now her stepsister would understand why Paige was willing to risk so much for him.

Paige settled into her seat for the ride home, a smile on her face.

"He seems like an okay guy," Jake told Katie as they drove home.

"Who?" Katie had been wrestling with the

problem of what to say to her parents, if anything, about running into Paige.

"That musician. The one with Paige."

"Oh. Philip. Yeah, I guess."

Jake glanced at her with mild curiosity. "What's up? Are you worried about Ben?"

"Sort of." She didn't want to explain about her parents' edict. They were getting home a little late, which meant he wouldn't be coming in the house. He'd take her as far as the front porch, kiss her good night, and then leave. So there was no danger of his revealing anything to her parents. "I don't think Ben knows about Paige and Philip. I don't think she's told him yet."

"*Is* there a Paige-and-Philip? How do you know they're not just friends? You know how Paige is about music."

I know, Katie thought, how she is about one *musician*! "No," she said thoughtfully "I don't think this is just a mutual interest in music. I think they really like each other."

Jake whistled through his teeth. "That's going to be rough on Ben. How come she hasn't told him?"

Because she's a lily-livered coward, Katie thought angrily. "I guess she's afraid of hurting him." Why was she sticking up for Paige? The favor would probably never be returned. Not in this lifetime.

"Has he said anything to you?" Jake wanted to know.

"Ben? No, not yet. But he might, if she doesn't tell him soon. And I don't know what I'd say if he *did* ask me what was going on. I am *not* going to lie to him for her."

Silence.

She looked over at him. She could barely see him in the darkness. "Jake! You don't think I should lie to Ben for her, do you?"

He shrugged.

That wasn't the answer she wanted from him.

"I just think," he said slowly and deliberately, "that this is between him and Paige. It's not your place to tell Ben about Philip. That's her job."

"But if she doesn't tell him, and he asks me. . . ."

"She'll tell him," he said confidently. "She will."

Well, she'd better, Katie thought fiercely. And she'd better do it soon. I wonder what she's going to tell Mom and Dad about tonight? If she comes into the house wearing that velvet skirt, with her hair all done up the way it was when I saw her, they're going to know she wasn't on any field trip. And where are the jeans she was wearing when she left the house?

Too tired to puzzle it all out, Katie lay her head on Jake's shoulder and closed her eyes. She'd worry about it later.

The jeans Katie had puzzled over were exactly where Paige had left them, to Paige's immense relief. She changed her clothes, released her hair, put the skirt back in the garage when she got home, and made it inside the house with ten minutes to spare. Telling Virginia Mae when she asked that the evening had been "fun," she claimed fatigue and went straight to her room.

There she found a thoroughly disgusted Katie Summer in pink pajamas, waiting for her. Perched on the end of her bed, she glared at Paige as their bedroom door clicked shut.

"What's *your* problem?" Paige asked impatiently. She stalked past Katie to her own corner of the room.

"You know very well what my problem is!" Katie said. "Now that I know what you're up to, what am I supposed to do about it?"

"Exactly what you were doing when you didn't know. Nothing!"

"But I *do* know! And that makes me . . . an accessory."

Paige laughed. "Katie, I haven't committed murder or stolen a car or robbed a bank. I've just told a fib or two, that's all. That's not a crime."

"What you're doing is wrong," Katie said quietly. "If Mom and Dad find out. . . ."

"And I suppose you'll make that your mission in life!" Paige said. "I'll bet you just can't wait to go running to them with your news."

"If I couldn't wait, would I be sitting here on this bed now, waiting for you? I've been home for twenty minutes, and I haven't said a word to them. I didn't even tell them I saw you!"

Paige sat down on the edge of her bed, facing her stepsister. "Look," she said earnestly, "I know I shouldn't be lying. I hate it." That was certainly true enough. She did hate it. "But what am I supposed to do? Your mother isn't being fair!"

"*My* mother?" Katie's neatly-trimmed brows rose. "You call her Mom, too."

"Well, I know I do, but she isn't *really* my mother." Paige's expression darkened with anger. "If she were, she'd understand how important Philip is to me."

"Oh, she'd understand, all right." Katie resented Paige's implication that Virginia Mae lacked understanding, forgetting for the moment those occasions when she'd thought the same thing herself. "She'd understand. She just wouldn't like it."

"Why?" Paige's voice rose. "He's one of the nicest people I've ever met. And she won't even give him a chance!"

"He's too old."

"Old, schmold! That's so stupid."

"My mother is *not* stupid," Katie said hotly, her own voice rising. "And if you're so sure you're right and Mom and Dad are wrong, why don't you just tell them?"

"I tried!" Paige said. "Believe me, I tried. They wouldn't listen!"

"Well, try again. I don't think you're fair, either, hiding things from them, sneaking around behind their backs."

Paige was about to respond when she was interrupted by a knock on the door. That loud knock was recognizable. Her father was at the door.

Paige and Katie exchanged glances.

"Girls, what's going on in there? Let me in, right now!"

Katie jumped up and opened the door.

William Whitman, still in his suit and tie, looked grim. "Okay, what's going on in here? I just got home from a meeting and I could hear the two of you all the way up the driveway! And who exactly is 'sneaking around' behind someone's back?"

CHAPTER 9

When no one answered him, William Whitman repeated his question. "I said, who's sneaking around?"

"Nobody," Paige answered, avoiding Katie's eyes. "And nothing's going on. It's just that this house needs another bathroom, that's all. Even if I get in there first, someone's always lurking around out in the hall, waiting to get in. It makes me crazy."

"The word I heard wasn't 'lurking,' " her father said skeptically. "It was 'sneaking.' And I can't believe you're arguing about who gets to use the bathroom first. I thought you girls had made peace about things like that."

Paige glanced at Katie. Her eyes were focused on the floor, her cheeks a deep pink. "We have, most of the time. But sometimes our schedules clash." She didn't add that the notion of her and Katie making peace struck her as ridiculous. But she found herself wishing it were true. Because if they had indeed made peace, she could count on Katie's silence about Philip. But the reality was, Katie could open her mouth at any time and toss Paige into hot water.

When Katie did open her mouth, she didn't mention Philip. "Sorry, Dad," she said, "I guess we got carried away." To Paige, she said, "You can have the bathroom. I'm tired. I'm going to sleep."

Her stepfather nodded. "Good idea. So is this settled for tonight? I don't want any more yelling."

"It's settled." Paige went to the closet to get her terrycloth robe. "But I still say we need another bathroom."

"Good *night*, girls. We'll discuss major repairs at another time." He left, shaking his head.

Later, in bed, with Katie already sound asleep, Paige's conscience plucked at her. What she was doing was no small infraction of the rules.

Katie had said, "Talk to Mom." Shouldn't Katie know Virginia Mae better than anyone? Maybe she was right. After all, Paige and Virginia Mae hadn't really discussed the situation the way they did most problems.

Having convinced herself that a lack of discussion was behind her problem with her stepmother, and optimistic about remedying it, Paige fell asleep.

Her opportunity came the following afternoon. Music greeted her as she walked into the house.

Virginia Mae was home, and she was probably in a good mood, because she was playing a show tune. She never played Broadway music when she was depressed or worried. So it was now or never. Taking a deep breath, Paige headed straight for the piano.

"Hi! Come and join me," her stepmother said, her fingers not leaving the keys. She was casually dressed in tan slacks and a cream-colored sweater and looked very relaxed.

Paige sat down on the piano bench. She listened quietly as Virginia Mae finished the piece, ending with a triumphant flourish. "There! Now, how about a duet?"

"Okay. But could we talk first?" Butterflies cavorted in Paige's stomach. But she couldn't put this thing off. It needed to be settled.

"Sure. What's up?"

She looked so calm, hands in her lap, a pleasant smile on her face. I, Paige thought, am about to wipe that smile right off her face. Because I don't have any choice.

"It's about Philip," she began.

There it went. No more smile. Not a good sign.

But Paige continued. "I just thought if I told you more about him, you'd understand how I feel."

"I'm sure he's a very nice young man, Paige. I never said he wasn't."

Encouraged, Paige began talking very rapidly. "Oh, he is! He's nice, and he's really smart and very considerate and — "

"And none of that makes any difference, dear."

It wasn't like Virginia Mae to interrupt. Another bad sign. "Because that doesn't change his age, does it?" She turned away from Paige and began leafing through a neat pile of sheet music on the piano.

She can't dismiss it like this, Paige thought. Not this quickly. "I know you'd like him if you got to know him. He's just the sort of person you seem to respect. He knows exactly what he's doing with his life. And music is everything to him." If that didn't do it, nothing would.

Nothing would, apparently, because Virginia Mae remained unmoved. Not even the tiniest trace of indecision showed in her face. But she did turn back to Paige.

"You're wasting your time," she said softly. "Your father and I discussed this further when we saw how upset you were. And we both reached the same conclusion: Right now, you are too young for Philip Grant."

Paige sagged against the piano. She knew when arguing with Virginia Mae was hopeless. Her stepmother wasn't going to give an inch.

Virginia Mae was looking at her with suspicion in her eyes. "Paige, I thought this was a closed subject. Why are you pursuing this issue now?"

A surge of anger took Paige's breath away. This was all Katie's fault. "Talk to Mom," she had urged. Well, she'd done that, and all she'd accomplished was raising suspicion in Virginia Mae. So much for Katie Summer's knowledge of her own mother!

Paige stood up. "I just thought," she said cooly,

"that if you knew more about him, you might change your mind. I was wrong. I'm sorry I bothered you." And before Virginia Mae could protest, she hurried out of the room.

I tried, she told herself as she climbed the stairs. I really tried. But it's hopeless. They're supposed to care how I feel, but they don't. And they aren't *listening*. So why should I listen to them?

When Philip called later, Paige told him she would be happy to go to a party with him late Saturday afternoon. Virginia Mae had answered the telephone, but she had mistaken Philip's voice for Ben's and had then left Paige alone to take the call in privacy.

Ben . . . she had to tell him something, and soon — before Katie felt sorry for him and blurted out the whole story.

But the next day, when Ben cornered her outside the journalism room, her determination to confess deserted her. There was no anger in his narrow face, only confusion.

"We need to talk," he said quietly.

"Now? Ben, I've got a million things to do in there!"

"So do I. But I won't be able to concentrate on any of it until you answer a few questions."

His eyes were serious. He was the first boy she'd dated more than a few times, the first who had kissed her as if he really meant it. She owed him some answers.

"Like what?" keeping her tone of voice light.

"Like why you never have time for me. Like

where you were last weekend. Like why you're not returning my phone calls." His voice became more intense. "Did I do something to make you mad?"

That was easy enough to answer truthfully. "No, of course not. I'm not the least bit mad at you."

He looked disappointed, and Paige immediately understood why. If she had been angry about some dumb little thing, he could have apologized and that would have been that. Now he knew it wasn't quite so simple.

"Then *what?*" he asked, bending his head toward her. "Why are you avoiding me? Why have things changed between us? C'mon, Paige, you owe me an explanation."

People passing them in the hallway directed curious glances their way. Paige ignored them. She realized she couldn't tell Ben about Philip just then, not there in a public place. "Ben, nothing's really changed. We're still friends."

"Friends?" He laughed, a brief, harsh sound. "Friends? Paige, we're more than just friends, and you know it. At least, we *were*. And I have a right to know what happened to change that."

When Laurie suddenly appeared, Paige could have kissed her. "Ben, c'mon," Laurie urged, tugging at Ben's elbow. "We've got work to do. Your love life will have to wait."

Pain flashed across Ben's face.

Paige saw it and hated herself. She knew he was thinking, *What* love life?

"I'll talk to you later," he said, his expression

telling her that he had hoped for more from their conversation. Head down, he followed Laurie into the journalism office.

"I have research to do at the library!" Paige called after them. She wasn't sure they'd heard her, but she began walking down the hall. Anything was preferable to following Ben into that room, even boring research.

I *will* tell Ben the truth, she thought as she hurried away. I will! Soon.

But Ben was tired of waiting for Paige to reveal the truth. His encounter with her in the hall had made it clear that whatever was going on in her life, she wasn't ready to share it with him. That made him nervous. What was she hiding? Hurt and confused, he made up his mind to seek out the only other person who might be able to enlighten him: Katie Summer.

He waited for her after swim practice, leaning against the wall outside the gym. When she came out, damp hair curling about her face, and saw him, her face flushed with anxiety.

Ben thought, She knows I'm here to ask questions. How can I talk her into giving me the answers?

Falling into step beside her, he said casually, "I'll walk you to the front door. Can't tell what evils might be lurking in these halls."

Katie forced a laugh. But she was being pushed in two different directions at the same time, and she found the tug-of-war nerve-racking. She knew what Ben wanted, and she didn't blame him. But she also knew that if Paige wanted Ben to have answers, she'd have given them to him herself.

"So," Ben said lightly, abandoning all pretense at subtlety so suddenly that he caught her unprepared, "who's the new man in Paige's life?"

"Well, I don't really know him. . . ." she began, and then stopped short. She had just admitted the very thing she'd intended to conceal. Paige would be furious!

She stopped and whirled to face him. "That's not fair! You tricked me."

"I didn't do any such thing." He shoved his hands into his jeans pockets. "Look, Katie," he said, looking directly at her, "we both know there's another guy in the picture, or Paige wouldn't be treating me like yesterday's news. So who is this mysterious stranger?"

Katie shook her head vigorously. "Oh, no, you don't. You're not dragging me into this. This is between you and Paige, Ben. You'll just have to talk to her."

Ben's face twisted. "I've tried. Do you think I would have come to you if I hadn't been desperate? She's not telling me anything. All I want is the truth. Is that so much to ask?"

"No. It's not." Katie wished fervently that she could remove that look of pain from his face. But the truth he seemed to want so much wouldn't do that. If anything, it would make his pain worse. She wasn't going to be responsible for that. "You have to get the facts from Paige, Ben. I'm sorry."

She turned and walked away, feeling a sense of disaster. Poor Ben.

"Poor Ben" watched her go. At least she'd confirmed the fact that there *was* another guy in Paige's life. And it wasn't someone from school, he was sure of that. So who was it? And why was Paige being so secretive?

His face a grim mask, Ben left the school.

CHAPTER 10

Just as Ben suspected, Paige was "otherwise occupied" that weekend. Getting out of the house Saturday afternoon for the party with Philip was much easier than she had anticipated. Miss Aggie had gone to the supermarket, Tuck had taken Scarlett to the park, and the two younger girls were shopping for new winter coats with their parents. Unfortunately, Katie remained at home, lying on her bed reading a magazine as Paige slipped into a simple, short black dress and black heels.

"What am I supposed to tell Mom and Dad when they ask where you are?" Katie asked, breaking a tense silence. "And where did you get that dress?"

"I've had it a long time. It's a jumper. I'm just wearing it without a blouse, that's all. And I shortened it. Looks good, don't you think?"

Katie sat up. "Paige! How can you be so

casual about all of this? You're lying to Mom and Dad; you're hurting Ben."

Paige kept her back to Katie, fussing with her hair at the dresser mirror. "Well, I tried," she said. "I took your advice and talked to your mother. She wouldn't even listen!"

"Then try again! You can't keep sneaking out of the house like this."

"I'm *not* sneaking. Not today. I don't have to, because no one's home. And Philip has to be at the hall by eight tonight, so I'll get home while Mom and Dad are at that dinner party the Wilsons are having." Thanks to the Wilsons, she wouldn't have to stop at the gas station. In and out of the house, free as a bird, with no one watching to see what she was wearing. Except Katie.

"I repeat, what am I supposed to tell them when they ask where you are? They *will* be coming home to get ready for that party. They'll want to know what you're up to."

Paige yanked her black velvet blazer from the closet and shrugged. "They won't even notice I'm gone."

"Oh, yes, they will. And I'm *not* lying for you."

"So, don't lie. Tell them the truth. I don't care anymore. Tell them whatever you please." Picking up her purse, she left, her heels rapping on the hardwood floor in the upstairs hall.

She doesn't mean it, Katie thought, rolling over onto her stomach and burying her head in her pillow. She doesn't really want me to tell them where she is and who she's with. And . . . even if she does, I'm not ready to cause that kind of uproar. Life won't be worth living in this house when Mom and Dad find out what Paige is doing. Why should *I* be responsible for that?

A friend at school whose parents were divorced and remarried had told her once, "The worst is when your folks fight about something you've done and the stepparent says, 'She's *your* kid, *you* handle it.' My mom likes to think we're all one big, happy family, and it makes her really crazy when my stepdad points out that I'm not really his kid." The girl had smiled wisely and added, "Sooner or later that will happen in your family." Then she had grinned. "But maybe it'll be Paige's fault."

Was this going to be the situation that set Virginia Mae and Bill against each other?

Not if they don't know about it, the answer came. Katie clenched her fists and promised herself that if they did find out, it wouldn't be because of words that came from her mouth.

Paige, standing in the center of a group of Philip's friends in a chic, mostly black-and-white apartment near the concert hall, wasn't thinking about stopping anything.

"I really like your outfit," Philip complimented her, "especially the red scarf. Just the right touch."

She had borrowed the scarf from Virginia Mae's dresser on her way out of the house. It wasn't the first time she had added to her wardrobe from her stepmother's, but it was the first time she hadn't asked permission. But then, how could she? Virginia Mae hadn't been home when she left. Philip was right: The scarf added just the right accent of color. And she didn't need the light in his dark eyes to tell her she looked every bit as nice as the older women at this party.

She was having a good time. All of the guilt and confusion she felt at home always oozed away when she was with Philip. And she was very aware that the old, shy, awkward Paige disappeared miraculously when she was with this group of people. She wasn't sure why. But it was wonderful. No one questioned her choice of ginger ale over cocktails. She had been afraid it would make people suspicious about her age. Instead, they laughed at her jokes, complimented her on her outfit, and asked her opinion of several different pieces of music. Being this happy made it impossible to think that what she was doing was wrong. How could it be?

"You look terrific," Philip said, smiling. "I wish I had more time to spend with you."

"I do, too." That was true. But the challenge of fitting any additional deception into her life seemed mind-boggling. She was doing a tricky tightrope act as it was. "But we're both pretty busy."

"Listen," he said suddenly, "I just thought of something. I'm guest-performing in Washington next weekend. Come with me?"

The invitation stunned Paige. People milled around them, laughing and talking, but she and Philip might as well have been alone on a distant planet.

She found her voice. "Washington?"

"D.C."

"Oh." That wasn't so far away . . . no, she was being ridiculous. She could barely manage to get away from the house for one evening. It would take a ton of miracles to get her away for a whole weekend.

"We'd have a great time," Philip said enthusiastically. "Have you ever been to the Smithsonian?"

"Once. When I was little." When my mother was alive and there was *no* stepmother in my life, Paige added silently.

"I could spend a year in there. You'll love seeing it now that you're older."

Not as old as you think, she thought, a bit sadly. Philip was extending this invitation because he thought she was as free to come and go as he was.

"Your folks won't mind, will they?" It was as if he'd read her mind. He grinned. "Washington *is* educational, you know."

Paige strangled a laugh. Wouldn't mind? Her folks wouldn't mind if she spent two days in Washington with the same young man she'd been forbidden to see for even a few hours? But then, of course Philip didn't know that. And he didn't know that she was only sixteen and he didn't know that the whole family was going to self-destruct if her parents found out what she was doing. But *she* knew.

"I'm sure they know Washington is educational," she said slowly. "But I don't think I can go, Philip."

Disappointment filled his handsome face. "Why not?"

She thought quickly. Philip wouldn't accept her family as an excuse. "I've got an assignment for the paper that's very involved. It's going to take a lot of research. I planned to do most of it next weekend." She hated that look on his face. Was she making *anyone* happy these days?

"Well," he said thoughtfully, "I don't want to interfere with your work. There isn't any way you could finish before next weekend? Maybe I could help."

"No, that's okay. It's something I have to do myself. Thanks, anyway," she said quickly.

Philip looked glum. "Well, I admire your dedication. But I'll miss you."

"It's only for one weekend."

"Maybe."

She looked at him, perplexed. "What does that mean?"

Philip took her elbow and led her into a quiet corner. "I may be invited to stay."

"In Washington? But you're guest cellist *here*."

"That's temporary. My agent sent tapes of my performances to the director in Washington. Now he tells me that if the weekend is satisfactory, for both me *and* the Symphony, they may want to take me on permanently."

"And you'd accept?"

"Well, I am looking for a permanent berth. There isn't a spot open here, and there is in Washington. It's that simple." He hesitated. "I wanted you to spend some time there so you could see how you liked it." His eyes were fastened on hers. There was no mistaking the tone in his voice. "Will you please just think about it? And if there's any way you can come with me. . . ."

She nodded. "I will think about it. I promise." His intensity was making her nervous. Things were getting more complicated than she'd intended.

Paige smiled at him. "Let's go filch some of those cute little sandwiches. I'm starving to death!"

Later, riding home alone on the bus, she thought about Philip's words when he had kissed her good night at the bus stop. "You're the best thing about Philadelphia, Paige Whitman." And he'd meant it.

Would he still feel that way when he found out that she wasn't who he thought she was?

"Georgetown University is a great school," he had told her. He still believed she was taking a year off between high school and college, like Jake was doing. And he wanted her to think about moving to Washington when he did. So they could still be together.

Paige groaned, and hid her face in her hands. You should have told him then, her conscience scolded harshly. The longer you wait, the harder it's going to be.

Paige was beginning to realize that was true of all lies.

When she got home, she went straight upstairs to change her clothes. Tossing her discarded clothing into the closet, she dressed in sweats and went back downstairs. Tuck was in the playroom with Megan and Mary Emily. Paige was invited to join their Jeopardy! game, but she needed to be alone to think and went into the kitchen to make a cup of tea.

When the phone rang, she thought it might be Philip, checking to make sure she had arrived home safely. But instead of Philip's voice, she heard Judy Belnap's.

"Some best friend you are! I called your house earlier and Miss Aggie said you were out with Ben. But I just saw Ben at the Seven-Eleven on the corner, and you were *not* with him. So what gives? Who *were* you out with?"

Paige wasn't willing to risk discussing Philip when she wasn't alone in the house. "It's early," she suggested, "so why don't we go out for a banana split? My treat!" She really did need to talk to someone about Philip. Who better than her best friend?

Informing Tuck of her plans, she hurried out of the house, grabbing a set of car keys as she left.

When their parents returned home and asked the whereabouts of their older daughters, Tuck answered, "Katie's out with Jake. And Paige went to meet Judy." Which completely satisfied Virginia Mae and Bill Whitman.

Katie had called Jake and said, "I really need to talk to someone. Are you busy tonight?"

"Not busy at all. Be right over," he'd said.

When he arrived at the house, Katie, suggested they go to the park. She immediately started talking about Paige. Jake put up a hand to stop her in mid-sentence. They were sitting on a bench, lighted only by a pale cresent-shaped moon overhead and old-fashioned streetlights scattered about the grounds. "Let's not get into that," Jake protested. "I told you, that's between Paige and Ben."

"I'm not talking about Ben," Katie protested, pulling the collar of her heavy red sweater tighter around her neck. "I'm talking about the family. Don't you care what happens to us?"

Jake hesitated, watching an elderly couple pass by with a collie on a leash. "Sure, I do. Your family matters to me. But your folks don't even know Paige is seeing this guy, do they?"

"No. But what if they find out?" Katie sagged against the back of the bench. "That's all I think about. I can't eat, I can't sleep. Or else I want to sleep all the time. Coach thinks I'm coming down with something, he said so. But all I'm coming down with," she added bitterly, "is a bad case of Paige-frustration! I've had it before, and I hate it!"

"You're getting ahead of yourself, as usual." Jake shifted on the bench, letting go of Katie's hand. "Personally, I don't see what's so terrible about what Paige is doing. So she likes this new guy better than she likes Ben." He shrugged. "It happens."

Katie didn't like the sound of that at all. Was he really that cool about Paige dumping Ben? Without even telling Ben why? Did that mean that if another girl came along, someone he liked better than Katie, Jake wouldn't think twice about dumping her. Well, there was a lovely thought!

Sometimes, she didn't know why she loved Jake Carson. This was one of those times.

"I think," she said stiffly, "that I'd better go home. It's colder out here than I thought it was." She stalked up the hill ahead of Jake. This is all Paige's fault, she told herself. And then, not for the first time, Why did Bill Whitman have to come fully equipped with a stubborn, pig-headed, rude, thoughtless, selfish, spoiled daughter? *Why*?

Jake kissed her good night on the porch and, when she didn't respond because she was too angry, he pulled her closer and kissed her again. Her anger melted because it felt so good to lean against him, to be in his arms, and to forget about family problems.

He smiled down at her as she pulled away. "Quit thinking so much," he said gently. "You'll get old before your time. Things will work out okay, you'll see."

She did feel better when she went inside. She was glad she had called him, after all.

CHAPTER 11

At breakfast the following morning, Virginia Mae came into the dining room looking disconcerted. "Has anyone seen my red silk scarf? The flowered one? I want to wear it with this suit, and I can't find it anywhere."

Paige sat perfectly still in her chair. She had intended to put the scarf back the second she'd entered the house the night before. What *had* she done with it?

Visibly annoyed when no one admitted knowing the whereabouts of her scarf, Virginia Mae took her seat at the table. "I'm sure it was in my scarf drawer," she murmured.

Paige bit her lip to squelch an inappropriate grin. But wasn't it just like Virginia Mae to have an entire drawer reserved for scarves? Did something horrible happen to scarves that were haphazardly tossed in with non-scarf clothing? Did they then become something less than one hundred percent scarf?

This isn't funny, she thought. You'd better come up with something pretty fast, because your stepsister is staring at you with that "I'll-bet-you're behind-this" look on her face.

"I think I saw that scarf on one of the shelves in the bathroom closet," she said. "It probably got stuck to a towel in the laundry. I'll run upstairs and check."

Virginia Mae shook her head. "That scarf is silk. I don't launder it. It goes to the dry cleaners." She smiled. "And if I did launder it, I certainly wouldn't toss it in with a load of towels."

Oh, no! Paige thought, annoyed. Silly me for not being educated in the proper care and feeding of silk scarves. Aloud, she said, "Well, you probably just took it off in the bathroom and left it there. I'll be right back."

The notion of her stepmother failing to put away her clothing was ridiculous and Paige knew it. But she also knew she wouldn't be able to breathe properly until that silly scarf was back where it belonged. She ran upstairs and into her room, where she pawed through the pile of clothing on the floor of her closet until she unearthed the missing scarf. The flowers on it had been mashed into a bouquet of wrinkles. But she'd found it. That was something.

Unwilling to return to the dining room, she called downstairs, "Found it! I put it in your drawer." Then she returned to her own room, where she launched a half-hearted attempt to create order out of her chaotic closet. When a knock sounded on the bedroom door, she called out a muffled, "Enter!"

"Paige," her stepmother's voice asked cooly, "do you have any idea how this scarf got so wrinkled."

Paige turned. Virginia Mae was holding the offending item in her hands. The look on her face was not one of amusement.

"Gee, I don't know, Virginia Mae. I guess it got tossed into the dirty laundry by mistake."

The proper name in place of the usual "Mom" brought a flinch from her stepmother. She's suspicious, Paige told herself nervously. She suspects that I borrowed the scarf, but she can't figure out why I didn't ask permission first, and she doesn't know why I don't confess right now.

In an attempt to defuse these suspicions, Paige joked, "Maybe Scarlett got hold of it. Or Binker."

Virginia Mae, after a moment's hesitation, let it pass. "All right. I was just wondering." After another brief moment, she turned and left the room.

She's going to go talk to Dad, Paige thought. She thinks he might know what's up because I'm *his* kid.

She waited. And ten minutes later the knock she recognized as her father's sounded on the door. She got up and went to answer it, grateful that Katie had had the good sense to remain downstairs.

Her father got right to the point. Wearing gray sweat clothes in preparation for his Sunday morning run, he sat on Paige's bed, his eyes on her face as she took a seat on the floor. "Paige, there isn't anything going on in your life that I should know about, is there?"

How could she have this conversation without lying? She did *not* want to lie to him. Did she have to? After all, she hadn't actually talked to him about Philip. Maybe the rules about her relationship with Philip had all been dictated by Virginia Mae, who had some really old-fashioned ideas. And she'd always been able to talk to her father, at least before the wedding in Atlanta.

"Well, there's this boy. . . ." she began awkwardly, her stomach churning. "The cellist I introduced you and Mom to at the charity dance after the concert that night, remember?"

He nodded. And she could tell from his expression that the subject of Philip had been discussed recently, no doubt with his wife. "Yes. The older boy."

Her father thought for a minute. "I guess you really liked this guy, hmm?"

Her heart leaped. Was he going to give in? Maybe she should have gone to him first.

But her hopes were dashed as quickly as they had arisen. "But you know," her father said cheerfully, "why we couldn't let that relationship develop."

Paige stared at the floor. He sounded so sure of his words. Like there couldn't possibly be any room for doubt about this particular situation. Which meant, she knew, that there was no room for argument. This was all a big waste of time.

"Paige? You do understand, right?"

When she didn't answer, he continued, "Your mom and I feel very lucky that we can trust you to obey us on this one, Paige. Some parents wouldn't have that luxury. Virginia Mae was a little worried. She sensed that you were very attracted to this older fellow. But I assured her you could be trusted. And frankly," he said with that charming smile that had been swaying juries for years, "that made me feel good. It's great to be able to trust my kids."

Paige cringed. His timing was really off.

"Dad. . ."

"Look, Paige," he said as he stood up, "just be glad we didn't let you get to know this young man better. Think how much worse you'd feel when you had to tell him good-bye. And you would have to, you know. Because you're too young for him."

Too young. Too old. Where were the rules about age written? Who made up those rules? Paige closed her eyes. Somebody's parents, for sure.

She remained sitting on the floor as her father prepared to leave. His gentle pat on her head infuriated her. I'm not four years old, she thought. Why can't you see that?

"I'm glad we had this little talk," her father said. "And remember, the best way to put something bchind you is to get on with your life. Concentrate on putting that young man out of your mind. You can do it, Paige. I'm counting on you. See you later," and to her relief, he left the room.

Paige circled her bent knees with her arms and lay her head on them.

"I'd be depressed, too, if I were you," Katie said as she came into the room. "But I've got to hand it to you about the scarf. You sure thought fast on that one. I could practically see the wheels in your head turning. You wore it yesterday with your black jumper, didn't you?"

Paige nodded, her back to Katie.

"Why didn't you just ask her if you could borrow it?"

Paige turned her head. "Because she wasn't home when I left. And even if she had been, I couldn't have asked. Because she would have asked me all kinds of questions about where I was going and who I was going with."

"That's the trouble with lying," Katie said in a maddeningly calm voice. "You get to the point where you can't even carry on a perfectly ordinary conversation."

"How would *you* know?" Paige couldn't imagine fresh-faced, open, honest Katie lying. Or needing to. Everything came so easily to her.

Katie, in jeans and a thick pink crew-necked sweater, sat on the edge of her bed, looking across at Paige. "One little lie becomes two or three, and then the whole bunch of lies becomes a great big one, like the giant snowball you get when you roll a little one down a snowy hill."

And this snowball, Paige reflected grimly, is

probably going to bury me. "Thanks for the lecture," she said. "You'll make a wonderful mother someday. You've got the lingo down pat." Then, "So what am I supposed to do? Stop seeing a really terrific guy for no reason at all?"

"There *is* a reason. Mom and Dad don't do things without a reason, and you know it, Paige."

She's just so glad it's not her, Paige told herself. She probably loves seeing me in trouble. "Well, it's a stupid reason!" She jumped up angrily and turned her back on Katie.

"What's stupid," Katie countered, "is that you're going to get yourself in a lot of trouble. And me, too, because sooner or later Mom and Dad will figure out that *I* know. Then I'll be in for it, too."

The knock on their door interrupting their argument made Paige realize they'd been shouting. And that knock had to be Virginia Mae's. Every knock so far that morning had meant bad news for her. Close to tears, Paige threw herself on the bed and hid her face in the pillow.

"Come on in!" Katie called, lying back against her own pillow. She hoped her mother wasn't coming to talk to Paige about the scarf, because Paige certainly wasn't in the mood. One more confrontation for her today and the room would go up in smoke.

Virginia Mae gave Katie a look that said, If you two don't stop this fighting . . . but all she said aloud was, "Paige, there's a telephone call for you."

Paige sat up. Philip? Or Ben? Or was it just

Judy, following up on their conversation of the night before? Judy hadn't been as understanding as Paige had hoped, because she really liked Ben. But she hadn't delivered a lecture, either. Paige was grateful for that much.

Paige didn't ask her stepmother who the caller was. All she said was, "Thanks" and hurried off.

When Paige had gone, Katie Summer held her breath. Was her mother going to ask what they'd been fighting about? If she does, she asked herself, what am I going to tell her?

But all her mother said, wistfully, was, "I wish you girls would stop fighting. It makes it very hard around here, for everyone." Then, with a sigh, she left, closing the door quietly after her.

CHAPTER 12

Paige wasn't as thrilled by the sound of Philip's voice as she might have been. She blamed that partly on fatigue and a bad mood, and partly on the fact that his invitation to meet him downtown that afternoon meant more maneuvering around her parents' questions.

"There's a movie I want to see," he explained, "and it's no fun going alone. It's a thriller. Everyone's talking about it, and I think you'd like it." He mentioned the title.

She'd seen it with Ben. And Philip was right, she had loved it. Which meant, she thought smugly, that he knew her pretty well.

"There's a showing at two this afternoon," he continued. "I can take the bus to your house if you'd rather not ride in alone, and we can ride back in together. On the other hand, if you meet me in front of the theater it would save time."

He really was thoughtful. Offering to come out

to the house. He had no way of knowing that that was the last thing in the world she wanted.

"No, that's okay," she said hastily. "It makes more sense to meet you at the theater." Katie and Jake never went to afternoon movies, nor did her parents. Megan and Mary Emily sometimes did, but Virginia Mae would never let them see this particular film. And Ben had already seen it. So . . . she wouldn't run into anyone to worry about. "I'll meet you at the theater at twenty minutes before two, okay?"

Now all she had to do was think of an excuse for leaving the house.

She passed Virginia Mae on the stairs. "Going to a movie," she said as she hurried past her stepmother. "Back before dinner."

"Oh." Virginia Mae turned to add a comment, but Paige had already disappeared inside her room.

In the living room a moment later, Bill Whitman asked his wife, "Who was on the phone?"

She picked up the newspaper and sat down on the sofa beside her husband. "Might have been Ben. Paige just said she's going to a movie. But she'll be back in time for dinner."

"Good." He smiled with satisfaction. "I had a talk with her earlier. Glad to see she's taking my advice and getting back with Ben, instead of moping over that cellist."

Virginia Mae frowned. "I didn't think she was moping all that much. In fact, I was a little surprised. She seemed to take our decision about that young man exceptionally well, didn't you think?"

Bill looked up from his paper. It was a beautiful crisp Sunday, the house was pleasantly quiet, and Paige had a date with Ben. Everything was close to normal, and he was in a good mood. He didn't want anything ruining it. A discussion about one or more of the children could do just that. "She was depressed enough when I talked to her this morning." He folded the business section with a sharp snap. "But Paige is smart. She knows it's a waste of time to fuss over something she can't change."

Virginia Mae found herself thinking, Since when? But she didn't say it. She wasn't any more anxious to see Bill's good mood destroyed than he was. "You're probably right," she said as he stood up. "You know her better than I do. She's *your* daughter."

She said it pleasantly enough. But Katie Summer, at that moment passing the living room, heard the comment and stopped in her tracks. Oh, no! This was exactly what she'd been warned about. She should have been prepared for it, but she wasn't. "*Your* daughter" — it sounded awful!

Caught up in her unhappy thoughts she didn't hear her stepfather tell his wife, "Going for my run, darling. Back in an hour."

But she did see him leave. And in her distraught frame of mind, it seemed to her that his sweat suited frame was stiff and unyielding.

This is all Paige's fault, she thought angrily.

She was trying to decide whether or not to approach Virginia Mae when Paige came running down the steps. She was wearing jeans and a blue sweater, but she had on more makeup than usual and a pale pink scarf around her head failed to hide the sophisticated way she'd done her hair.

"You're meeting Philip, aren't you?" Katie whispered.

"That's none of your business." Paige moved toward the door, anxious to leave before Virginia Mae popped out of nowhere. But Katie blocked the exit.

"Does it interest you at all to know that Mom and Dad are fighting because of you?"

Paige stared at Katie. "That's ridiculous. How can they be fighting when they don't even know I'm *seeing* Philip?" Her dark eyes narrowed. "Or do they, Katie?"

"I never said a word. But they're not stupid, Paige. They probably figured it all out by themselves."

"No, they didn't. I talked to Dad this morning, and he didn't know a thing. I would have been able to tell."

Virginia Mae chose that precise moment to walk into the foyer. She had such a sweet smile on her face that Katie instantly realized she must have misinterpreted what she had overheard. Flushing with embarrassment, she stepped away from Paige.

But Paige wasn't thinking about what Katie had told her. She was too busy being terrified that

Virginia Mae would notice the makeup and the arrangement of braids pinned to the top of her head.

But all her stepmother said was, "Enjoy your movie, dear," without even glancing Paige's way. "Say hello to Ben for me," and she went on up the stairs.

The comment flooded Paige's cheeks with scarlet. "I never said I was going with Ben," she whispered as Katie stared at her accusingly. "Anyway, you were way off-base. If they're fighting, I'll eat this scarf I'm wearing."

"Well, maybe they're not right now. But they *will* be. Just wait and see. And it'll be *your* fault!"

"Oh, stop it," Paige said easily, and left the house.

Katie stood in the foyer, clenching her fists. When she was positive that Paige was long gone, she headed for the park. Fresh air would clear her mind faster than anything else. And she'd be avoiding any questions Virginia Mae might have about why her daughters continued to be at each other's throats so often. Questions she wasn't ready to answer, even though she was furious with Paige. No, she thought as she ran down the steep stone steps, this is not a good time to have a conversation with my mother.

She went to the park instead.

When Ben Collins arrived at the house fifteen minutes later, only Virginia Mae was there to answer his doorbell ring. She frowned when she opened the door and saw him standing on the porch.

"Ben? Did you and Paige get your signals crossed?"

"Excuse me?" He liked Paige's stepmother, but right now she was confusing him. "I just dropped by to see if Paige was home."

"But I thought she was with you. Weren't you going to the movies this afternoon?"

Ben shook his head. "I haven't talked to her. Did she say she was going somewhere with me?"

Paige's stepmother thought for a minute. "No, you know, now that I think about it, she didn't. I just assumed — "

"She probably went with Judy. Listen, I'll catch her later, okay? Thanks. See you, Mrs. Whitman." He ran down the steps as if he didn't have a care in the world.

Nothing could have been further from the truth. Because Ben didn't believe for a second that Paige was with Judy. He had always trusted his own instincts. Under ordinary circumstances, he would have believed that there was every chance Paige really was with Judy. But the way she'd been acting lately combined with her stepmother's belief that she should have been, at this moment, out with Ben, made him suspicious.

A suspicion that was confirmed less than ten minutes later when he spotted Judy Belnap walking through the park, a grocery bag in her arms.

He had never been as angry with Paige as he was at that moment. Seeing Judy had cleared up a few things, to his complete disgust. It was clear that Paige had dumped him for another guy. And that was bad enough, especially since she hadn't been straight with him about it. That didn't seem at all like the Paige he knew, but now he understood why. His visit to her house had proved to him that the other guy was someone her parents disapproved of. Otherwise, why pretend she was seeing Ben when she wasn't? The guy was on her folks' "no-no" list, that was for sure.

The worst part was Paige's letting them think she was with him. She was using him.

Whoever the guy was, this new relationship was one Paige had to keep secret. No wonder Katie Summer hadn't told him anything. He'd never get anything out of her.

He'd try Tuck. Tuck would sympathize with being dumped and then used as an excuse for some secret relationship.

He couldn't help wondering what the problem was. Maybe the guy was a real thug, some wasted creep who rode a motorcycle and lived in leather. But what would Paige be doing with someone like that? Then what? What was it about this guy that her parents refused to accept?

Deciding to corner Tucker Guthrie as soon as possible, an angry but not-quite-so-confused Ben drove home.

Paige and Philip had a few minutes together after the movie before she had to catch her bus.

"Thought anymore about next weekend?" he asked as they walked, hand-in-hand, toward the bus stop. The sun had disappeared behind clouds, erasing what had been a beautiful day, and a sharp wind had arisen. Paige was glad they were both wearing heavy sweaters. "The Washington trip, I mean. I was hoping you'd changed your mind. It would be a lot more fun if you went with me."

Paige had never been so strongly tempted. Seeing Washington, D.C. with someone as bright and interesting as Philip would, she was certain, be the best experience of her life. Not to mention the most romantic. And if she didn't go, what would the weekend hold in store for her? Two days of tension and bickering with Katie and listening to her parents tell her how right they'd been about not letting her see Philip.

But how could she go? What excuse could she possibly give for an entire weekend away from home? If she were Katie, she could pretend she was off to Atlanta to see old friends. But she had lived in Philadelphia all of her life. She had no out-of-town friends.

I know, she thought as they walked the quiet downtown streets, that going on this trip would convince Philip once and for all that I'm every bit as mature as he is, that I'm free to make my own decisions.

Looking over at him, striding along self-confidently, his dark hair blowing in the wind, she wondered if there might not be a way. "I really want to go," she said impulsively, and loved the way a smile lit his face at her words. "Let me think about it, okay? I'll let you know if it's at all possible." At least this way, even if she couldn't go, he'd never suspect that it had anything to do with her parents.

"You mean it? That would be terrific!"

He really wanted her company on this trip. That meant a lot to her. He must find her very interesting and attractive or he wouldn't be anxious to spend two whole days with her.

"I'll try. I'll really try," she said.

She was so excited during the bus ride home and so preoccupied with the puzzle of how to get away for the weekend that she almost forgot to stop at the gas station to remove her makeup and adjust her hair. She remembered just in time.

CHAPTER 13

If Katie had known Ben thought she was aiding Paige in her ongoing deception, she would have been shocked. She had never intended to help Paige, not in this. Helping Paige recover from that terrible car wreck was one thing. *That* had made her feel good. But this was something entirely different, and *none* of it made her feel good.

Deciding that she was tired of wrestling with the situation alone, she took it to her friends. "I have this pal in Atlanta," she told them at lunch one day in the school cafeteria. "She has a sister two years older than her who met this older guy. Her parents think he's too old for her and they've said she absolutely, positively can't see him. But she's seeing him anyway."

"That's so romantic," Lisa said.

Katie shot her an annoyed look. "Anyway, my friend wrote to me last week. She's desperate. She said she's afraid her parents will find out not only that the sister is seeing this guy behind their backs, but that my friend *knows* about it. And they'll lock her in her room until she's thirty-five."

"How old is the guy?" Diane, the more logical of Katie's three best friends, wanted to know.

Katie decided to adjust the facts just a bit, to protect the guilty. "Twenty-three."

"And the girl?"

"Seventeen."

"Older guys are so much more . . . mature," Lisa said dreamily.

Diane laughed. "Well, *that* makes sense!" Then she returned her attention to Katie's problem. "He's too old for her, Katie. Really. She's still in high school, right?"

Katie nodded.

Diane continued, "Well, what I want to know is, what does *he* see in *her*? Why isn't he dating girls his own age?"

Katie studied her napkin. It was decorated with little white ducks with blue gingham bows around their necks. "My friend's sister is pretty, especially when she dresses up. And she's smart. And interesting." Was she actually saying those things about *Paige*? Well . . . they were true enough, weren't they?

Sara took a sip from her milk carton while Lisa daydreamed and Diane thought about the situation. "A sister can't tell," Sara said firmly. "Life in that house would be a disaster if the younger girl finked." She looked directly at Katie as she spoke. "She'd better butt out."

She knows, Katie thought with certainty. Sara

knows I'm talking about me and Paige. But that was okay, because Sara would never tell anyone. She wasn't the gossipy type.

"I agree," Diane said, nodding. "It's between the older sister and her parents, period."

Lisa nodded then, reluctantly. "Yeah, I guess you're right. Finking stinks! Friends just don't do that to each other."

I never said they were friends, Katie thought. I said they were *sisters*. Not the same thing, is it?

Later, walking to class, Katie thought how much simpler things would be if Paige really were just a friend, instead of stepsister. That way, if Katie ever *did* tell, it wouldn't involve family and the results wouldn't be something she'd have to live with twenty-four hours of every day of her life.

Her friends were right. Finking on Paige would cause more trouble than Katie was ready to handle.

When Ben finally caught up with Tuck, he was standing outside the gym with several friends. "Tuck? See you for a minute?"

Reluctantly, Tuck left his companions. If there was was one thing he hated, it was getting an earful of other people's romantic problems. He had enough of his own. He had no idea what was going on between Ben and Paige. He only knew that Paige seemed jumpier than usual, that there was more tension than ever between her and Katie, and that Ben hadn't been hanging around the house lately. "What's up?" he asked, hoping Ben wouldn't tell him.

Going to Paige's stepbrother was as hard on Ben as it was on Tuck. Approaching Tuck was a measure of his desperation, and he wasn't comfortable with it. Too casually, he asked, "Paige said anything to you about me? About us?"

Tuck forced a laugh. "You've got to be kidding! You must have us mixed up with the Cleaver family. Only I'm not Wally and Paige isn't The Beaver. Lately, the only thing she comes to me for is to borrow money." He said it a bit more harshly than he'd intended. So they hadn't become one big, happy family. So what? Maybe there wasn't any such thing. Maybe that sort of family was just a figment of some television writer's imagination.

Ben managed to laugh, but his heart wasn't in it. Tuck was his last resort. Did he really not know anything?

Sensing that he'd disappointed Ben, Tuck added, "The only thing I've noticed is that Paige seems really jumpy. Not eating much, that kind of stuff. Like she's got something heavy on her mind."

"Well," Ben said lightly in an effort to hide his feelings, "it's not me!" Something heavy on her mind? Didn't that sound like what he'd suspected? That Paige was seeing someone against her parents' wishes?

"I could ask her about it if you want," Tuck offered. He really didn't want to get involved. But he liked Ben, and the poor guy looked really miserable. "See what's going on. She'll probably tell me to mind my own business, but it's worth a try."

Ben thought for a minute and then shook his head. "No, that's okay. I don't want her to think I've asked you to check up on her. I'll just wait it out, I guess. Thanks, anyway, Tuck." And he turned and left.

Tuck watched him go. Anger at Paige filled him. Whatever was going on in her life, why couldn't she have laid it all out for Ben? He didn't want any part of this business. He had problems of his own. The friends he'd collected at this school made a very small group, and Jennifer Bailey hadn't fallen into his arms the way he'd hoped she would.

But if Paige were up to something she shouldn't be, it could affect the whole family. They needed another major crisis like they needed smallpox.

Okay, he told himself as he headed for his locker, keep your eyes and ears open. Knowledge is power, as they say. If you can find out what's going on, maybe you can fix it.

His suspicions about Paige deepened at dinner that night.

"How's Ben?" Bill Whitman asked his daughter.

The question caught the three older children off-guard. Paige's cheeks flushed rosy red. Katie choked on the water she had been in the process of swallowing, and Tuck sat up straight, glancing at Paige with interest.

"Oh, he's fine," Paige managed in a matter-of-fact voice. Only the whiteness of her knuckles wrapped around her water goblet gave her away.

"Haven't seen much of him around here lately. You two didn't have a falling-out, did you?"

Avoiding a direct answer to the question, Paige said, "He's been awfully busy lately. Lots of newspaper stuff, I guess."

Her father smiled. "You tell him I said, all work and no play makes for a very dull life."

Paige knew what he was doing. He had told her that the best way to get over Philip was getting on with her life. He had meant getting back to Ben, she knew that. And now he was a little worried because she didn't seem to be doing that. Was he suspicious about that movie Virginia Mae had thought she was seeing with Ben? Her stepmother had told her later that day that Ben had stopped by. But she seemed to assume Paige had been with Judy. What had she said to Paige's father?

"Right, Dad. I'll be sure and tell him. May I please be excused?"

"Paige, you haven't eaten a thing," Virginia Mae pointed out.

"I'm not hungry."

"Mom," Mary Emily drawled plaintively, "how come I have to finish everything on my plate and Paige doesn't?"

"Because you're little," Paige responded, trying to smile. "And you won't grow if you don't eat. I've already got my growth." Looking at her father, she added, "I've also got a beast of a headache. So please, may I be excused? I'll eat something later, I promise."

"I suppose so, if you're really not feeling well. But you haven't been eating much lately. You're not on some silly new diet, are you?"

Paige was, and always had been, pencil-thin. "Dad!"

"Okay, okay! You're excused."

Tuck watched Paige leave the dining room. She had said Ben was too busy for her. But he had just talked to Ben and the impression Ben had given him was that it was Paige who had no time for *him*. So who *was* she spending time with?

And then a switch clicked in Tuck's mind and he remembered the musician. The guy Paige had met at some party after a concert. He played one of the larger instruments . . . cello, wasn't it? He'd overheard his mother talking to Bill about the guy. Philip something. But they'd nixed that relationship in a hurry, hadn't they? Because the guy was too old.

It all made sense now. Paige's nervousness, Ben's confusion, the daggers Katie kept sending Paige's way. He knew Paige well enough to guess that if she really wanted to know this guy, telling her she couldn't see him would be like waving a red flag in front of a bull. He'd bet his next date with Jennifer that Paige had mutinied on this one. And that Katie knew. And that Ben, definitely, didn't.

He waited until Katie had gone upstairs. If they were in on this together, he wanted to tackle them together. What he couldn't understand was why Katie would support Paige in a crazy deal like this. It wasn't as if they were the best of friends. Most of the time, they weren't friends at all.

When he knocked on their door, Katie answered it. Her lips were tight at the edges, as if to hold something in that she didn't want released. She might be in on this with Paige, but she wasn't happy about it. She'd be on his side, then. He knew Paige well enough to know he'd need someone on his side.

He closed the door and leaned against it. Paige was standing by the long, narrow window overlooking the side garden, looking out into the darkness. Katie busied herself with a collection of small perfume bottles on the dresser.

"I want to know what's going on," Tuck said. "I don't care which one of you spills it, but I'm not leaving this room until someone confesses."

Paige turned to face him, a grin on her face. "Spills it? Confesses? Too many detective shows on television, Tuck. You'd better try sit-coms for a while."

"Not funny, Paige. Just tell me why you're acting like you're carrying secrets for the CIA, and why you're making Ben's life so miserable, and I'll leave."

All traces of a smile left Paige's face. "None of that is any of your business, Tucker Guthrie. I don't pry into your personal life. So please do me a favor and get out of my room."

"It's my room, too," Katie said quietly, turning away from the dresser to face both of them. "And I think Tuck should know what's going on."

Paige glared at her. "Why should I tell him

anything? This hasn't got a single thing to do with him."

In the face of her anger Katie took a step backward. But not Tuck. He refused to back down. "I thought you liked Ben," he said slowly and deliberately. "If you don't, why can't you tell him that to his face, instead of leaving him hanging like this? He doesn't have a clue about what's going on."

"And you do?" Paige leaned against the windowsill, crossing her arms in front of her. Her cheeks were red and her eyes were flashing darkly, almost black. "I *do* like Ben. And I can't believe you were actually discussing me with him. Were you?"

Watching them, Katie bit her lower lip. This was exactly why she'd kept quiet about Paige and Philip. Telling could only mean trouble for the whole family, like right now. If Mom and Dad heard these two fighting, they'd be in this room like a shot, demanding to know what was going on. "Lower your voices," she urged.

"Answer me," Paige demanded of Tuck, "did you discuss me with Ben Collins?"

"He came to me," Tuck answered, obeying Katie's order to lower his voice. "He's hurt and confused. You owe him an explanation, Paige, and you know it." His eyes focused on Paige's. "Is that musician really worth all of this?"

Paige's body jerked upright, her eyes nearly piercing Katie. "You *told*! I *knew* you couldn't be trusted!"

"I didn't — "

Tuck interrupted Katie. "She never told me a thing. It wasn't that hard to figure out. Mom and Dad will, too, soon enough. So will Ben. That's what I meant when I asked you if this guy was worth it. A lot of people are going to be really ticked off with you, Paige. You're just asking for it. What goes on in this house affects me, too," Tuck said, his voice cool.

Guilt and anger and frustration made Paige say whatever came into her head. "This isn't even really your house!" she cried. "It's mine and my father's!"

Katie gasped and Tuck's face drained of all color.

Paige was sorry immediately. "I'm . . . I'm sorry," she stammered, stricken by the look of pain on Tuck's face. She knew Tuck had never felt at home in this house, with this combined family, and she had just reinforced those feelings of not belonging. "Really, I didn't mean it."

"Yes, you did!" Katie whispered. "You *did* mean it! You've been thinking it every day since we moved in. And Tuck and I knew it. We're not stupid, Paige." Turning to Tuck, she said clearly, "You were right, Tuck. Paige *is* dating that musician. Mom and Dad told her he was too old for her, but she's seeing him, anyway."

Then, for a strained moment, no one said anything. Tears in her eyes, Paige walked over and sat down on her bed. Tuck shot her a look of such contempt that she felt a sudden chill. Then he whirled and left the room, slamming the door so hard, the tiny glass perfume bottles on Katie's dresser clinked against each other.

"Well," Katie said wearily, "I hope you're happy now, Paige."

Paige stared at her with eyes glistening with unshed tears. Happy? Everyone but Philip hated her. Or would, when they found out what she'd been doing.

If it was the last thing she ever did (and maybe it would be), she was going to figure out a way to go to Washington with Philip. She had to get out of the house!

CHAPTER 14

With Katie Summer and Tuck aligned against Paige, the atmosphere in the big yellow house became increasingly strained. Meals were quieter than usual, the uncomfortable silence broken only by the chattering of Megan and Mary Emily and Virginia Mae's gentle prodding of the older girls to "eat something."

The older girls weren't hungry. Katie, especially, recoiled at the sight of Miss Aggie's expertly-prepared dishes. The sunny, cheerful dining room had become, for her, a gray place, where she had to face Paige across the table. Having Tuck on her side proved to be no consolation at all. That had only accomplished an increase in the family's misery quotient. Now Tuck was glaring at Paige as much as Katie was. He obviously hadn't forgiven Paige's cruel remarks, and Katie didn't blame him. Paige had been really rotten. And knowing that she was genuinely sorry didn't help. That wouldn't erase the cruel words she'd spoken to Tuck.

The increase in tension didn't escape their parents' notice, just as Katie had known it wouldn't. Her stomach did a loop-the-loop when Bill looked up from his meal one night and said, "Okay, guys, what's the problem here? Am I wrong or are the three of you acting like gladiators about to face each other in the Colisseum?"

Virginia Mae nodded. "I've noticed it, too. You don't even seem to be speaking to each other."

Tuck's laugh was a mirthless one. "Maybe some people don't feel free to carry on a conversation," he said bitterly, "in a house that doesn't belong to them."

Paige flushed scarlet, while Katie went as white as her linen napkin.

"Megan, Mary Emily," Virginia Mae said hastily, "you've finished eating. You're excused. Run upstairs and get at your homework."

"I don't have any," Mary Emily answered cheerfully.

"Me, neither," Megan echoed.

"Then you may watch television. Go on now."

"C'mon, M. E.," Megan said, getting the message. "Let's go watch 'Wheel of Fortune.' We'll see who can guess the puzzles first."

When they had gone, Bill leaned back in his chair. "Explain that remark, please, Tuck. The one about the house not belonging to you."

Paige fingered her napkin nervously. She had no idea what Tuck was about to say, but it couldn't be good. If he told the truth, her father would want to know the reason behind her attack on Tuck, and she couldn't very well tell him. Would Katie? After all, Katie was Tuck's *real* sister.

Tuck wrestled briefly with the idea of forgetting the whole nasty mess. He could pass off his remark as having no meaning at all, just something that had slipped out. Then they could all go on their merry way. Merry? But Paige's words echoed in his brain: "This is *your* house! It's mine and my father's!"

But Bill was his father now, too. Sort of. In a way. So didn't that make this his house, too? Maybe he owed it to himself to find that out.

"Is this or is it not," he asked deliberately, ignoring the fact that Paige was obviously holding her breath, "my house, too?"

Paige sagged backward in her chair.

Katie bit a trembling lower lip.

Virginia Mae and Bill stared in disbelief at Tuck. "Of course it's your house, too," Bill answered. "Why on earth would you ask a question like that?"

Tuck scraped his chair backward and stood up. "Then maybe you'd better explain that to your daughter," he said, "because she doesn't seem to think so." Leaving his unfinished meal on the table, he turned and left the room.

"Oh, Paige," Virginia Mae said softly, hurt in her face as she looked at her stepdaughter.

"I'll handle this," Bill said brusquely. "Paige! In the living room! This minute!"

Throwing her napkin down in a gesture of defeat, Paige stood up. Head down, she followed her father out of the room.

"Katie?" Virginia Mae asked her daughter. "Why would Paige imply that Tuck didn't belong in this house?"

Katie was tempted to say, Because she's a terrible person. But she didn't really believe that. Not all of the time, anyway. Paige had said it because Tuck had criticized Paige for seeing Philip. Katie couldn't very well tell her mother that, could she?

"I guess she was mad," was her only answer. Every muscle in her body wound itself into knots, waiting to see if Virginia Mae was going to pursue the issue.

Her mother sighed heavily. "Honestly," she said in exasperation as she stood up, "I don't understand why you can't all get along. You're all intelligent, sensitive people. You could learn a lesson from Megan and Mary Emily, it seems to me. Look how well they get along."

Katie hated being compared unfavorably to her younger sister. Mary Emily was just a kid, without responsibilities. Small wonder she didn't cause any trouble. Besides, Mary Emily wasn't being asked to get along with someone as prickly as Paige.

"I try," she defended herself. "And so does Tuck."

Her mother looked skeptical. "Yes, well, it can't *all* be Paige's fault. It takes more than one person to carry on a war." Filling a large wooden tray with dishes, Virginia Mae took them into the kitchen, letting Katie off the hook for the time being.

As satisfying as it would have been to eavesdrop on Paige's lecture from her father, Katie decided she had no stomach for that sort of thing and went upstairs instead. Paige could just flounder alone in her own sea of disgrace. She had it coming.

"You've had this lecture coming to you for some time now," Bill Whitman said to his crestfallen daughter. "You never spend any time with this family anymore. And when you do, what comes out of your mouth isn't what anyone wants to hear. What exactly did you say to Tuck about this house not being his? And how could you say anything so cruel? You know he's had trouble adjusting here."

"I didn't mean it," Paige said, without volunteering her exact words to Tuck.

Her father stood at what she thought of as his customary "lecture podium," in front of the fireplace, tweed-jacketed elbow resting on the white mantel. "And I apologized. Right away." Her lower lip thrust forward. "Tuck was just being stubborn and wouldn't accept my apology."

"I don't blame him."

Paige lowered her head. "That's no surprise," she said softly, "you never blame him."

"What was that?"

"Nothing."

Her father frowned and told her to look at him. She obeyed. "Look, Paige," he said sternly, "I can understand your arguments with Katie. Two girls about the same age, thrown together suddenly whether they wanted to be or not, sibling rivalry, that's understandable. But what ever possessed you to attack Tuck? He's done nothing to hurt you."

Except interefere in my life, Paige argued silently. Aloud, she said meekly, "I know. I *said* I didn't mean it. Why is everyone making such a big deal about it?"

"Because it was a cruel thing to say to a boy who isn't sure *where* he belongs anymore." He thought for a minute before adding, "Paige, I think everyone has been more than patient with you. But sometimes I think you're not even trying."

Paige's mouth quivered. "You just told me the other day that you were proud of me. Did you change your mind already?"

"No, I haven't changed my mind. I meant what I said. But we're talking about something different here. We're talking about your refusal to accept Virginia Mae and her kids as part of this family."

"Oh, I accept *her*. Most of the time. When she's not living in the Dark Ages."

Virginia Mae's husband's mouth became a thin, straight line. "Paige," he warned, "you're walking very close to the edge here."

She ignored the warning. "I accept her," she repeated. "But I want Katie and Tuck off my case. They're not my keepers."

The sudden curiosity in her father's eyes told

her she had said too much. In one more second, he'd be asking her why two of the Guthries were on her case. She backtracked hastily. "I mean, I know I was rude to Tuck and I'm sorry. I'll apologize again, if you want." She softened her tone of voice. "I guess I'm just not used to having all these people in our house, Dad."

"This is their house, too, Paige." His tone of voice had *not* softened. "And I expect you to remember that every single minute. Have you got that straight?"

Mute, she nodded. He hated her. She could tell. All that stuff he'd handed her about being proud of her was just so much garbage. Virginia Mae had probably talked him into that speech, to make up for squelching her relationship with Philip.

"And yes, I do want you to apologize to Tuck again. And you'd better make sure he knows you mean it." He paused. "Understood?"

She moved her head in a barely perceptible nod.

"Paige? Do you understand me?"

"Yes! I do. Now, may I please be excused? I have a lot of homework." Standing up, chin high, she avoided his eyes.

There was a measure of weariness in his voice as he said, "Yes, you're excused, Paige."

Fighting tears, she walked, stiff-legged, out of the room. Why was it, she wondered as she climbed the stairs, that if they were one big, happy family, only her father lectured *her*, while presumably Virginia Mae lectured only *her* kids?

What kind of togetherness was that? Shouldn't family include the bad as well as the good? Only . . . where, exactly, was the good?

"I am really sorry for what I said," she told Tuck a few minutes later. She had gone straight to his third-floor retreat upon leaving her father. First things first. "I honestly didn't mean it. Of course this is your home, as much as it is mine."

Tuck stared at her with unforgiving eyes. "Your dad made you come up here, didn't he?"

She was grateful that the overhead light in the narrow passageway outside of Tuck's room was dim. He probably couldn't see how embarrassed she was. "Yes. He did." No point in pretending otherwise. Tuck wasn't stupid. "But I would have apologized, anyway. What I said was hateful. I wish you'd just chalk it up to a case of nerves and forget about it. Please?" Life in this house would be extremely unpleasant if Tuck remained openly hostile to her.

Tuck leaned against the doorway to his room. "Tell you what," he said lazily, "I'll make a deal with you. I'll let you off the hook on this one if you'll clue Ben in on this other guy, this musician."

Paige's mouth dropped open. He was blackmailing her? "You want me to tell Ben about Philip? I thought you liked Ben."

"I do. That's why. You're not being fair to him and he doesn't have any idea what's happened. You have two choices here, Paige. Wise up Ben, or deal with your dad when I refuse to speak a civil word to you when he's in the room."

Some choice! "I was going to tell Ben the truth, anyway," she said. "I was just waiting for the right time."

"Yeah, right. Like when elephants learn to type, right?"

"Tomorrow. Honest." She refused to allow him the satisfaction of feeling that he was controlling her decisions. "I was going to tell Ben tomorrow."

"Yeah, well, do it." He grinned. "Then I'll think about forgiving you." He stepped back and closed the door.

Fuming all the way to her room, Paige was in no mood for Katie's anxious, "Is everything okay now?" as she entered and threw herself across her bed.

"Are you serious?" she asked, glancing at her stepsister. "How could everything possibly be okay? All I want to do is get out of this house!" She turned her face away, curling up in bed and yanking the comforter up to her chin.

Thinking, We were all happy in Atlanta, weren't we, Katie got up and went to call Sara. She needed to talk to someone who would listen with a sympathetic ear. That certainly wasn't Jake, who hadn't called her once since they'd argued about whether or not she should tell her parents about Philip, and it certainly didn't include anyone who lived in the house with her. It would have to be Sara.

Paige approached Ben the following afternoon with dread. She had thought about inviting him to the house for their talk, but was afraid someone would overhear when she told him about Philip. It would have to be at school. She felt sick inside. Lately, he had been treating her with a cool nonchalance that barely masked his true feelings. Had it been her choice, she would have left things that way. It seemed preferable to risking his anger. But Tuck expected her to tell him the truth, and her father expected Tuck to forgive her. One wouldn't happen without the other. She had no choice.

They had already put the paper to bed for the week so their work load was light. Ben was sitting at his desk when she approached him, the sleeves on his plaid flannel shirt rolled to the elbow, his legs up on the desk top.

"Could I see you out in the hall for a minute?" she asked.

His thin, sensitive face filled with hope. "Yeah, sure. Nothing much to do here." He jumped up and followed her out of the room. In the hall, he faced her eagerly.

He thinks I'm here to fix everything between us, Paige realized, her heart heavy in her chest. And I do *not* want to do this. But I have to. "Ben," she began quietly, "I'm sorry I didn't talk to you about this sooner, but I didn't want to hurt you."

Behind his glasses, the hope in his eyes faded.

"It's just that I didn't know exactly how to say it."

"You mean how to tell me about the other guy?"

Shocked, she stared at him. "What . . . what other guy?"

"Oh, come on, Paige. You must think I'm really dense. I know there is someone else. And I know it's someone your parents aren't thrilled with, because when I went to your house the other day, your mother thought you were out with me. You must have wanted her to think that. The question is, what's wrong with the other guy?"

Paige gave in, then. He already knew, which meant she was spared the effort of telling him. "They think he's too old for me. It's so stupid!"

"How old *is* he?"

"He's only twenty-one! And Virginia Mae acts like that's positively ancient!" Caught up in her own anger, Paige missed the disheartened look on Ben's face at her failure to deny the existence of another guy.

"And what about us?" he asked bluntly.

Paige's head jerked up. "Us? Oh. Well. . . ."

"If you think I'm going to hang around like a lost puppy waiting for a kind pat on the head from you, think again." His tone of voice had hardened noticeably. "I've got better things to do with my time."

When she said nothing, because what could she say, he added bitterly, "And I'm really disappointed that you've been doing this to me, Paige. You should have told me the truth right away. I guess I had you figured all wrong."

She struggled to protest, No, you didn't! But the words remained stuck in her mouth.

"Just do me a favor, okay?" He backed away from her, his face flushed. "Don't use me as an excuse when you go to meet your new boyfriend.

I don't like being used." Giving her one last look loaded with contempt, he turned on his heel and strode back into the journalism room.

Paige couldn't have followed if a fire had been raging at her heels. She couldn't face being in the same room with Ben. Following her impulse to get away, she hurried outside, and ran down the stone steps.

She had almost reached the bottom step, head down, when a familiar voice called out, "Well, what a neat surprise! What are *you* doing here?"

She looked up into the dark, penetrating eyes of Philip Taylor Grant.

CHAPTER 15

For one horrible, stunned second, Paige thought her charade had been destroyed. She was on high school property. She was carrying an armload of high school textbooks. She was wearing very little makeup, her hair was hanging loose around her shoulders, and she was wearing a typical high school outfit: jeans, a sweater, and sneakers. She couldn't possibly look a day older than her actual age.

But Philip didn't seem to notice. The expression on his handsome face remained pleasantly surprised, without a hint of suspicion. "You look cute," he said. "And I repeat, what are you doing here?"

Cute? That sounded dangerously . . . young. "I'm doing some research on high school textbooks. We're planning a feature on what the taxpayers of this fine city are getting for their money." That sounded good, didn't it? "How about you? I never expected to run into you all the way out here."

"There's a kid here who's thinking of trying for Juilliard. The Symphony Director sent me out here to talk to him. I just finished."

"Oh." He looked wonderful, in jeans and a red sweater under a tan suede jacket. But someone she knew could come by at any moment. "Want to go get coffee? You're not in a big rush, are you?"

He smiled, turning her knees to peanut butter. "Not now."

She was careful to pick a restaurant that Harrison students regarded as boring. When they were seated opposite each other in a maroon fake-leather booth, he said, "Thought any more about the Washington trip?"

"Of course I have," she said lightly, toying with her napkin. "When are you leaving?"

"Tonight. At seven. On the train." He took her hands in his. "You sure you can't make it? It won't be the same without you." Another bone-melting smile.

A wave of longing swept over Paige. Why wasn't she just a few years older? She leaned back against the booth. "It sounds like so much fun." And fun wasn't exactly spilling out of all the nooks and crannies of her house.

"Well," he said, his eyes on hers, "if you decide you can tear yourself away from your newspaper work, throw a few things in a suitcase and catch me at the train station. And bring your dancing shoes!"

She had never wanted anything so much in her life. What if she just went? Just walked out of the house, met Philip at the train station, and went to Washington with him? She could deal with the consequences later. What could they do to her that would be worse than missing out on this trip? Ground her forever? If Philip moved to Washington permanently she wouldn't feel like going out, anyway.

She was being ridiculous. There was no way she could do this. Her parents would never forgive her. Things were bad enough at home without the added crisis of a disobedient, missing daughter. And if she left an explanatory note, her father would come after her. He'd drag her away from Philip and all she'd be left with was a horrendous case of humiliation.

"I don't know Philip, but you have a great time," she said sincerely as their coffee arrived. "And miss me, okay?"

"No problem."

Paige could tell he meant it.

She left him half an hour later at the bus stop. Unmindful of a handful of waiting passengers, Philip kissed her good-bye. Missing him already, she returned the kiss with all of the yearning she felt inside. The waiting passengers smiled and applauded.

Paige wasn't embarrassed. She was feeling nothing but sadness. Watching Philip climb aboard the bus, it took every ounce of strength she had to keep from boarding it with him.

She waved at the departing bus until it was out

of sight. Then she walked home alone, kicking savagely at fallen leaves as if they were responsible for her unhappiness.

Hoping she could avoid confronting any member of her family, she closed the front door quietly as she entered the house. She intended to slip up the stairs and into her room unnoticed.

What stopped her was the sound of her name. It was Virginia Mae's voice, coming from the kitchen. Since no other voice responded, Paige relalized her stepmother was in the middle of a telephone conversation. And the subject of that conversation was . . . Paige.

Tiptoeing to just beyond the kitchen door, Paige shamelessly eavesdropped. She needed to know why her stepmother was discussing her and with whom.

"Well, I'm really worried about her," Virginia Mae's voice said clearly. "There is something going on there." A pause. Then, "No, I haven't talked to her about it. Didn't you?"

Paige made a face at the celing. She was talking to Paige's father.

"I think Katie and Tuck know something about it, but I can't very well force them to tell me. That wouldn't be right."

Paige smelled roast beef cooking. Was Miss Aggie in there with Virginia Mae? Or was she upstairs putting laundry away, which would mean she could show up on the stairs at any second? And where were Mary Emily and Megan? It would be excrutiatingly embarrassing to be caught eavesdropping.

"The second I can get her alone, I'm going to insist that she tell me what's going on. Whatever it is, I think she'll confide in me when she realizes I mean business. Do you have any objection to that plan?"

Object, object! Paige mentally telegraphed to her absent father.

"Good. That's settled, then."

Shaking her head, Paige sagged against the wall. She heard Megan and Mary Emily laughing upstairs, and the faint sound of rock music from Tuck's third-floor room. That left only Katie, who was probably in their room.

Then she forgot about all other family members as Virginia Mae said, "You don't think it's about that young man, do you? You remember, that musician? The one we told her she couldn't see?" A definite edge crept into her voice as she added, "An order I, if you remember, thought she was taking too well?"

Stunned, Paige's mouth dropped open. Why couldn't her father have married someone *stupid*?

"It may not be that at all," Virginia Mae's tone was more conciliatory now, "but if it is, I'm going to put a stop to it right now. Paige has got to accept the fact that we mean business on this one. And if she has been seeing him against our wishes, she will have to be disciplined. Do you agree?"

Of course he would agree. Paige was sure of that. She decided not to hang around for the rest of the conversation. She'd heard enough. Turning, she ran out the front door and to the nearest pay phone. With trembling fingers, she dialed Philip's rooming house, hoping that he hadn't left yet.

He hadn't. The sound of his voice soothed her.

"I'm coming with you," she said, a bit shakily. "I'll meet you at the train station in half an hour."

Philip was delighted. "See you there," he said cheerfully, and she hung up.

When she got back to the house, she slipped in as quietly as she had earlier. Even in her rush, she was careful to skip the stairs that creaked, jumping them like stepping-stones in a stream.

Hoping fervently that Katie wasn't in their room, Paige threw open the door and rushed straight to her closet.

Katie was sitting on her bed, reading.

"Girls, Tuck," Virginia Mae called up the stairs just then, "I just talked to your father."

Yeah, I know, Paige thought grimly, yanking clothes from hangers.

"He's been held up. Dinner won't be until seven."

Paige, her back to Katie, smiled. Now no one would question her absence until after the train had pulled out of the station. When she called Philip, she'd been so upset she hadn't even thought about dinner. It would have created a serious problem. Now she could just forget about it.

"What are you doing?" Katie asked, frowning.

"Nothing. I'm doing absolutely nothing. Go back to your book." She tossed her beige canvas bag on her bed and began stuffing sweaters into it.

"Where are you going?" Katie swung her legs over the edge of her bed and sat facing Paige's side of the room. "Are you sleeping over at Judy's tonight?"

"Yeah, right. Judy's." Dancing shoes, Philip had said. She pawed around underneath her bed until her hand hit black suede. One shoe, then the other. She pushed them underneath the sweaters, but not before Katie had spotted them.

She sat up very straight, back rigid. "Paige! You wouldn't be taking those shoes to Judy's." Her blue eyes opened wide. "You're not going to Judy's, are you?" She stood up. "Paige, tell me where you're going."

Paige ignored her. The black velvet skirt and blazer, but what blouse? Her white one was in the laundry.

"Paige, you're not . . . you're not going somewhere with Philip, are you? No. You're not that stupid."

The blue blouse would have to do. Blue looked okay with black, didn't it? Well, she certainly couldn't ask Katie's advice. Blue it was. In it went.

"Paige, you tell me where you're going."

Should she take an evening purse? If they really did go dancing, she'd look like a fool with her old shoulder bag. Paige grabbed a clutch purse from her drawer and thrust it into the canvas bag.

That was the last clue Katie Summer needed. "I don't believe this," she said slowly, sinking down on her bed. "You're going somewhere with that musician person."

Where had she put her sunglasses this time?

"Paige, you can't do this!"

Paige refused to look at Katie. "Oh, yes, I can. And you can just keep quiet about it. It's none of your business."

"It *is* my business. Mom and Dad will freak out! Paige, you'll ruin everything!"

Paige whirled, then, to face her. "Ruin everything? What is there to ruin? You already did that, you and your family, by coming here." Words that had been straining for a long time to be released spilled forth. "Everything was just fine until you showed up. Now, my father doesn't like me very much. Megan spends all of her time with Mary Emily, and she likes you more than she likes me. And I have a stepmother who thinks girls should play with dolls until they're old enough to vote!"

Shocked, her skin pale, Katie defended her mother. "She's not like that and you know it, Paige!"

Paige knew she had gone too far. "Okay, okay. Forget it. But I'm doing something *I* want to do for a change, and nobody's going to stop me. So just butt *out*, Katie."

"What am I supposed to tell Mom and Dad when they ask where you are?"

Paige zipped her bag closed and threw on a wool tweed blazer. Picking up the bag and sliding on her shoulder bag, she turned to look at a shaken Katie Summer. "Just keep them entertained with that cute little drawl of yours," she said bitterly, "and they won't even notice I'm gone. Now, I've got a train to catch."

With one last, quick glance around the room, she took a deep breath and stalked past Katie. A moment later, while Katie watched in horrified silence, the door closed with a final-sounding click.

Paige was gone.

CHAPTER 16

Katie's first thought as the door closed was, She'll never get past Virginia Mae. But a minute later, she heard the front door slam shut. And when she ran to the front window, there was Paige, running down the steps, canvas bag in hand.

She was tempted to let it go. Let Paige go off with Philip, let their parents find out, let the whole family disintegrate from the resulting explosion. She could just crawl back into bed like a bunny burrowing into its hole and find peace and safety there. Let Paige deal with the mess she was making for herself.

No. She couldn't leave it alone. Because the mess Paige was making involved all of them. They were a family, whether Paige accepted that or not. Okay, so they weren't like television families with their quick, easy solutions to every dilemma. And Virginia Mae wasn't everyone's real mother and Bill wasn't everyone's real father. What *was* real, though, was that they all lived together now, and if that didn't make a family, Katie didn't know what did.

She couldn't let Paige do this. There was too much at stake.

Jumping up and grabbing a jacket, she ran out of the room. She pounded up the few stairs to Tuck's room. Rapping sharply on the door in order to be heard over his stereo, she shouted, "Tuck, let me in! Hurry *up*!"

Despite the music, he'd been asleep. His hair was askew, his eyes heavy lidded.

"Wake up!" Katie commanded. "Paige is about to do something really stupid. We've got to stop her!"

Tuck rubbed his eyes. "Why? Let her do it. Then we'll have the fun of watching her get punished."

"She's not just getting a bad grade on a test or staying out past curfew, Tuck. I said *really* stupid. Now, c'mon, grab a jacket and don't argue. I'll fill you in on the way."

He groaned, but her tone of voice left no room for quibbling. He did as he'd been told.

They met Miss Aggie on the stairs.

"Now, where are you two off to? Dinner's coming up as soon as your father gets home. And where's Paige? She never came home from school."

Oh, yes, she did, Katie thought. Aloud, she said, "We're just going to pick her up now." She hoped like crazy that that was the truth. "Tell

Mom, okay? We'll be back in time for dinner."

As promised, she filled Tuck in on the details as he drove toward the train station.

"Wow!" he commented when she'd finished, "What are Mom and Bill going to say?"

"That's just it," Katie said earnestly as Tuck maneuvered through heavy evening traffic. "I don't want them to know. If we can convince Paige to come back home with us, they don't need to be told, do they? Unless she suddenly feels like telling all. I don't think Mom even knows Paige was in the house at all this afternoon."

Concentrating on his driving, Tuck made no comment.

"And I don't think she hates us," Katie added thoughtfully. "I think she likes this guy a lot, and she can't stand it that Mom and Dad blitzed the relationship. So she's getting back at them."

"Maybe." Tuck spotted a gap up ahead and aimed for it. "But methinks her idea of bliss right now is getting as far away from us as she can."

Katie shrugged. "That's too bad. She's just going to have to learn to live with us. Like we have to live with her."

"*If* you can talk her into giving up this little junket."

"I can. I will. I'll get her back home even if I have to tie her up."

"Bring any rope?"

"Forgot it. I'll use my scarf. Or my socks. Or Philip's tie, if he's wearing one."

Neither of them laughed.

At the train station, they searched the crowds

frantically. Since Katie had no idea what Paige's destination might be, she could only hope the departing couple hadn't made it yet to their assigned gate. If they were still milling around in one of the waiting areas, Katie and Tuck had a chance of spotting them.

But there was no sign of a tall, slender girl with long, dark hair toting a canvas bag, or a handsome young man with a cello case.

"Remember the proverbial needle in the haystack?" Tuck said. A man in a hurry smacked Tuck's elbow, knocking him off-balance. "It's Friday night, Katie. This place is mobbed. We have about as much chance of finding those two here, as we do of convincing Mom and Bill that Paige was suddenly stricken by a wild desire to spend the weekend at Judy's."

Katie couldn't give up. "We have to try the platforms. We'll do them one at a time. Maybe we'll get lucky."

"Katie — "

"No! We *have* to do this! I told Miss Aggie we were bringing Paige back with us, and that's what we're going to do. Come on!"

They dashed from gate to gate, breathless, and frustrated by the crowds. "Look for a cello case!" Katie urged. "He'll have it with him. Musicians never trust their instruments to baggage handlers." She had no idea how she knew that, but she was postive it was a fact.

It was. And it was the cello they spotted first, on the platform where passengers destined for Washington, D. C. gathered.

"There!" Katie shouted, grabbing Tuck's elbow. "There it is! And there's Paige." Relieved to notice no train waited on the tracks, Katie dragged Tuck through the crowd until they faced an astonished Paige.

She's going to hate me, Katie thought calmly. But maybe she'll get over it. Maybe someday, a million years from now, she'll be glad we stopped her.

She nodded toward Philip, knowing she must be a frightening sight, all sweaty and red-faced, hair every which way. "I'm Paige's sister," she said politely. "Would you mind if my brother and I talked to her for a minute?"

"I don't have anything to say to you," Paige whispered. "Go away!"

The platform was noisy and Philip hadn't heard her whisper. "Sure," he told Katie and Tuck. "The train isn't here yet. Paige, go ahead."

Unwilling to create a scene and arouse suspicion in Philip, Paige allowed Katie and Tuck to pull her aside.

"What are you *doing* here?" she hissed, her face a mask of barely-suppressed rage.

"You're coming home with us right now," Katie said, wasting no time.

"You're crazy! I'm not doing any such thing. I'm going to Washington with Philip. And you two are going to turn around right now and march out of here. You're going back to that house without me."

"No," Tuck said, stepping forward. "We're not.

You've caused plenty of trouble since Mom and Bill got married, Paige. But this one tops them all."

"You didn't even leave them a note!" Katie accused. "If I hadn't figured out what you were doing, no one would know where you were. They'd be out of their minds with worry."

Paige tossed her head impatiently. "Don't be ridiculous. I wouldn't put them through that. I'm going to call them when we get to Washington. I'll tell them I'm just fine, and they don't have anything to worry about."

"Oh, great!" Tuck looked at Katie, a cynical expression on his face. "That should do it, right, Katie? She can just tell them she's in another city with a guy she's not even supposed to *know*, and everything will be just great!" Turning to Paige, his words heavy with disgust, he said, "Get real, will you, Paige? Why didn't you just plant a bomb under the living room sofa and be done with it? The effect would be the same."

"Go home," Paige said flatly, and walked away, back to Philip. She immediately began to chatter animatedly, as though Katie and Tuck had never arrived.

The train pulled into the station.

Katie had no choice. She knew Philip couldn't possibly know Paige's real age. That explained the extra makeup and fancy hairstyles Paige adopted whenever she left the house to meet him. Besides, he didn't look like the sort of person who would be dating a high-school student.

She took a deep breath and let it out. She looked at Tuck. They had discussed this in the car. "It's time for Plan B," she said, her voice low.

"Right. Let's go."

They approached the couple together. When Paige saw them, her dark eyes filled with anger, but there was fear there, too.

She knows what I'm going to do, Katie thought, and she's scared. I don't blame her. It's going to be sticky for her.

She almost changed her mind, imagining how she would feel if she were caught in a mammoth lie to Jake. Mortified.

Then the prospect of Paige getting on the train strengthened her resolve.

"Philip," she said quietly, "Paige is only sixteen years old."

Paige's face went scarlet.

Philip stared at Katie, then at Tuck. Then he laughed, a friendly laugh.

Katie had expected that. "No, it's true," she persisted. "She's only one year older than I am, and I'm fifteen. And a half. She goes to the same high school I do."

Philip's smile slowly disappeared. He tightened his grip on the cello case and shook his head. "No. That's ridiculous. What is this, some kind of joke?"

Katie said nothing. She had given him her message. It was up to him to decide what to do with it.

Philip looked at Tuck.

"It's true," Tuck said. "She's my stepsister and

I can tell you for a fact that she's not seventeen, yet."

Slowly, Philip's head turned toward Paige. The truth was written in her face but still, he waited for a denial.

Color flared in her cheeks. She gave Katie and Tuck a look of such loathing that Katie took a step backward, bumping into Tuck, who stood his ground.

There followed a long, painful moment of awkward silence. Philip kept his eyes on Paige's face. All she could manage, finally, was a weak, "Philip, don't listen to them."

His mouth grim, he took her hand and pulled her off to one side, leaving the cello case with Katie and Tuck. The platform had cleared of all but a few passengers. Alone with Philip, the impatient chug-chugging of the waiting train ringing in her ears, Paige stood white-faced and silent, head down.

"Sixteen?" Philip's voice was full of disbelief. "Sixteen? Paige? Is that true?"

What was the use? "Yes," she murmured, "it's true."

Philip's shoulders slumped. He shook his head. "It can't be." He thought for a minute. "When I met you that first night, at the party, you looked at least eighteen, if not older."

Paige lifted her head. She had to look up to meet his eyes. They were darker than ever, under dark eyebrows drawn together in a perplexed frown. "That first night," she said, tears trembling on her eyelashes, "that was clothes and makeup and hair. A lot of girls my age look older than they really are."

She could see what a difficult time he was having absorbing this unexpected information. He looked like someone had just pulled the ground out from under his feet. And it was her fault. No, it was Katie's fault, Katie's and Tuck's. She would never forgive them.

"But why didn't you tell me later? You must have known I assumed you were older."

There was no point in any more deceit. She might as well be honest now, no matter how humiliating it was. "I wanted to tell you. But I knew if I did, you wouldn't be interested anymore."

His lips tightened. "Well, you've got that right. I don't date sixteen-year-olds, Paige."

Although her vision was blurred by the tears in her eyes, she could see the change in expression on his face as he went from shock and disbelief to acceptance of the facts and, she felt, disapproval.

"Paige, your parents didn't want you seeing me, did they? That's why you made a point of meeting me downtown. That started right after I met them, didn't it? So they don't even know you've been seeing me, do they?"

She shook her head. She couldn't bear the look on Philip's face. It was a look of betrayal. Of disappointment.

Trying to muddle through his shock, Philip said slowly, "So you're not at all who I thought you were, are you? Never mind the age thing.

That's bad enough. And I should have asked, I guess. It never crossed my mind that I needed to. But worse than the age thing is that the Paige I thought I knew, wouldn't do all of the lying you must have had to do. What about the newspaper job? A figment of your imagination?"

"High-school paper," she murmured.

"Ah."

Watching from a distance, Katie actually felt a pang of sympathy for Paige. She was the very picture of misery.

Seeing the look on Katie's face, Tuck said, "She's got it coming to her."

"I know."

Tears streamed unchecked down Paige's cheeks. She was powerless to stop them. "Philip," she said, her voice husky, "I've never done anything like this before. I hope you'll believe that. I don't like lying. And I especially hated lying to you. I'm sorry. It all just sort of . . . happened. Please don't hate me."

"I believe you. Because I hate to think that I could be so wrong about a person. And I don't hate you. I could never hate you. But I have to tell you, I feel incredibly stupid."

The train made an irritable sound and a conductor shouted something about boarding.

"I guess," she said softly, "that if you come back here, you won't call me."

"I'm not coming back," he said decisively. "I wasn't sure until now. If they don't offer me a permanent spot in Washington, I'll have my agent look elsewhere."

Paige wiped at the tears on her face with the sleeve of her blazer. The fabric scratched. "Because of me? Is that why you're not coming back?"

He pulled a white handkerchief from an inside jacket pocket and gently dabbed at her tears. "Maybe. In a way." The conductor shouted again for passengers to Washington to get on the train. Philip reached out again, this time to touch Paige's cheek with one hand. "I told you, Paige, you were the best thing about Philadelphia. Being in the same city with you and not being able to see you doesn't strike me as a fun way to run my life. And I told you, I don't date sixteen-year-olds."

So it hadn't been just her parents who objected to the age difference. Philip would have, too, had he known.

"I won't ever see you again, will I?" she managed to ask.

He took a moment to walk over to Tuck and collect the cello case Tuck had been holding upright for him. When he returned to Paige, he said, "Who knows? Maybe I'll be back this way one day."

She hesitated. "I'll be older then," she said, hope in her voice.

And he managed a very small laugh. "Yes, I guess you will. That's the way it works." He looked down at her for a moment. The disappointment in his face, the betrayal, had been replaced by sadness. "Promise me one thing."

"Anything."

"Promise me you won't change too much. It wouldn't hurt you to grow up a little, but don't change a lot, okay? I . . . I really like you just the way you are." Then he turned and climbed the train steps and disappeared.

Katie and Tuck left Paige alone until the last train car pulled out of the station. But during the painful good bye, Katie had seen that Philip really cared for Paige. Which made it easier to understand the motives behind her stepsister's behavior and now, her pain.

When the last car had disappeared from sight, Katie walked over to Paige. She touched her arm. "Paige, c'mon. We have to go."

Paige, her face tear-streaked, eyes swollen and red, faced Katie and Tuck. "I will never forgive you for this! Never!"

Making no reply, they led her out of the station.

On the way home, Paige sat alone in the back seat, staring out the window, every now and then audibly sniffing back a tear.

She has to forgive us, Katie told herself as they neared the house. Because if she doesn't forgive us, we can't be a family. Maybe, when all of this was behind Paige, when she'd returned to her normal life and forgotten Philip, maybe then she'd forgive them.

Paige continued sniffling, loudly, hoping it made Katie feel guilty. Paige stared at the back of Katie's blonde head. In some part of her mind that could still be logical, Paige knew that Katie had done the right thing. She knew that sooner or later Philip would have found out the truth and that her parents would have been badly hurt by her going off with Philip. Maybe someday she would be able to tell Katie that, but for now she just said again, "I'll never forgive you for this!"

Katie leaned toward Tuck and got some comfort from the warmth of his shoulder. "Yes, you will, Paige. Someday you will forgive us both."